OTHER BOOKS PUBLISHED:

Il était une fois my caillou
(published by Editions du Santal, New Caledonia in 2005 in French under the author's real name 'Peter Appleton'.)

My Secret Profession
(published by Jojo Publishing Australia—2005)

The Buggerum Intrigue
(published by Interactive Publishers—Australia 2007, Highly Commended IP Picks).

A Teaspoon of *Giggles*

PAUL STERLING

PARTRIDGE
A Penguin Random House Company

ISBN:	Hardcover	978-1-4828-9761-6
	Softcover	978-1-4828-9760-9
	Ebook	978-1-4828-9762-3

To order additional copies of this book, contact
Toll Free 800 101 2657 (Singapore)
Toll Free 1 800 81 7340 (Malaysia)
orders.singapore@partridgepublishing.com

www.partridgepublishing.com/singapore

A TEASPOON OF GIGGLES

An Anthology

This collection of inter-related short stories concerns the inhabitants of a fictitious region of Victoria, Australia, the Lamington Peninsula. They invite the reader to laugh at their antics, although a couple of murders, a bungled burglary, a reluctant emigrant and a sweet love affair add a little spice to the theme.

Many of the protagonists work for businesses owned by the infamous Sabatini family, usually because they have little choice in the matter. They still enjoy life to its fullest and manage to share marvellous memories and inspiring adventures

THE DOCTOR'S WIFE

Angela Smith was proud to be the doctor's wife, although she was a little different to most of her counterparts. She had what is called a 'generous' figure, she never went to the hairdresser, she bought many of her clothes at Target[1] and she drove a Mazda 323 that squeaked and coughed and moaned and probably suffered from arthritis. She did not live in a Lexus-infested suburb of Melbourne, but in a regional city called Sutton Vale where virility is often measured by the size of the bull-bar or the number of spot lights on a Kingswood ute. She knew that some people, behind her back, said that she looked frumpy and plump, but she did not care a toss. Her darling husband loved her just the way she was: 'comfortable' and 'cuddly'.

Angela enjoyed a secret life. Each day, when the sun went down behind the Hills Hoist, after a couple of glasses of Sauvignon Blanc, her husband could become quite libidinous. He encouraged her to buy dresses or blouses with big, big buttons, because he loved 'examining' her by unfastening those buttons very, very slowly while she pretended to resist, although her defensive actions were always hampered by a terrible bout of giggles that his exploration always

1 Her friends call it 'Tarjay" which sound more chic

seemed to provoke. He told her often how proud he was to have a married a beautiful white Australian girl.

Kofi, the husband from heaven, was born in Ghana. He was a very handsome African, with smiling eyes and sparkling teeth and a grin that made many of his female patients fear an onslaught of arrhythmia when he looked at them. He was educated in London and his diplomas were from the most reputed schools of medicine in the Old Country, and usually outshone those of his colleagues, in his wife's modest opinion.

She also believed that he was a very good doctor, one that listened, nodded, smiled reassuringly and offered kind words of advice and encouragement. His prescriptions were short and appropriate. He always spent too much time with each patient, so that he was always behind schedule. Patients in the waiting room sometime looked at their watches, sighed loudly or shuffled their feet with impatience. But they knew that while they are waiting somebody was receiving an overdose of tender loving care.

In the early days Kofi had his own practice and Angela was his receptionist. It was not easy for him, being a doctor with a black face in a regional town in Victoria. But there was a shortage of general practitioners in smaller communities, so people came, first reluctantly, then with more assurance. Angela was very proud when Mrs Watting came out of his surgery one day, with a great smile on her face to whisper those wonderful words.

"He is such a good doctor that you forget he is black!"

She was very proud when the Sutton Vale Medical Centre asked him to join them. He shared receptionists, accountants, billing clerks and nurses with other perfectly white doctors. The computer software often reminded him that he always spent more than the regulatory eight minutes with each visitor, but the patients loved him. Suddenly out of a job, Angela started to work from home as an ambitious but rarely successful freelance journalist and photographer. She adamantly refused offers to become a 'marketing consultant' selling incontinence knickers, magic bras or smart phones to people who do not really have any use for them.

Kofi had three passions in life: his wife, his patients, and the Arsenal Football Club, also known as the Gunners. But Angela was sure that he was never tempted to unbutton Arsene Wenger[2] shirt with the enthusiasm he showed with hers.

His favourite patients were his pensioners. They knew that time was of essence. As the years passed by, clicking over like the odometer of a Ford Zodiac, they knew that there was still much left to do, and that they were running out of time. Kofi had an elderly patient called Peter, a typical old man, a little stooped, unsteady on his feet, but with a brain in overdrive. He told Kofi that when he died he would be getting answers to many questions that were nagging away at him every day.

"Such as what?" the doctor asked him one day.

"Does God exist?" Peter explained. "If so, does she look like Pamela Anderson or Margaret Thatcher? Do pit-bull terriers, lawyers, politicians and real estate agents all go to heaven? And, more importantly, will I go upstairs, enjoying perfect health, playing Scrabble with some scantily clad nymphs; or will I be in the basement, checking my blood pressure every day and playing poker with a team of guys with tattoos, bulging biceps and Harley Davidson bikes. Oh, and another thing. Will I still have prescriptions?"

Kofi laughed. Peter admitted to having OFAD or Old Farts Attention Disorder. He told the doctor one day that when time was short it seemed silly to waste away the hours sitting in a doctor's waiting room. He saw several reasons.

Firstly, from a health point of view, it was about as dangerous as sitting next to a cholera plantation[3]. Secondly, because all the magazines talked about royal weddings, how to grow orchids, baking a chocolate cake, how to fold table napkins, canoeing down the

---

2 Trainer of Arsenal, a Frenchman, naturellement!

3 If such a thing exists.

Murray and other totally boring subjects. Thirdly, because most of the hot news they announced had happened ten years ago. Fourthly, because sitting there gave him time to worry that Kofi was going to prescribe probes, needles, scans, and other humiliating inspections, always in those parts of his body that he considered very personal, and inevitably undertaken by a smileless[4] nurse with a three-day moustache and big, big muscles And fifthly, because there were far more important things to do elsewhere.

He would be happier if Kofi told him that he should be eating more steak, more sausages, drinking more beer and wine, having sex only when he felt like it, peeing as often he likes[5] and watching footy matches on Foxtel, on a couch, munching crisps for hours. Peter was not overweight, he was simply resplendent!

Peter died just after the footy final. He was picking up a prescription and suddenly disappeared from the pharmacist's sight. They found him on the floor in front of the counter, quite dead, with a big smile on his face. Kofi examined the body of his old friend and issued the death certificate.

"Why was he smiling?" Angela asked, when he told her of his patient's departure.

Her husband grinned.

"I think he probably met Pamela Anderson," he said wistfully.

---

4 This will be in the dictionary next year

5 Without discussing whether it is in a straight line or not!

THE COLONEL LOSES A BATTLE

Paul Hutchinson could not hide his happiness. He wore all day on his face that smug look of self-satisfaction that showed that he was pleased with himself. He was delighted to know that those who considered themselves his friends believed that he had completed an exemplary career as an officer in the regular army and that he had seen heroic and patriotic action on various fronts.

"When I was in Libya," was a typical introduction to one of his boring and self-ingratiating anecdotes. Nobody actually knew what he was supposed to have done in Libya because his acute modesty and the reputed discretion required by those having served in in Special Forces prevent him from discussing those possibly harrowing experiences. Suffice to say that his friends called him Colonel Hutchinson with that tone of respect in the voice that meant so much to him. His first wife knew that he had only reached the rank of corporal in the Army Catering Corps, and that his only heroic action had been losing a fight with a Free Belgian fighter pilot in a pub in Aldershot, Hampshire, when he was still living in the U.K. She was in fact the barmaid who had provoked the fight, but she had taken that secret to the grave with her.

Moving to Sutton Vale and its beautiful Durrington Lake had allowed Colonel Paul Hutchinson to preserve and embellish his spectacular military career. His civilian activity, as assessor for the Globe Providence Insurance Company, was less spectacular. He was supposed to be an expert in assessing vehicle accident repair costs, but, as one reputed panel beater put it, 'bloody Hutchers didn't know the difference between a bumper bar and an ignition coil.' His social ambitions were often thwarted, such as his failure to be admitted into the Royal Victoria Club.

"I don't care who you pretend to be," John Walsh had told him very loudly in the bar of the club, when, as a guest, he had broached the subject of becoming a member. "We do not grant admission to upstarts and immigrants!"

He had also been very embarrassed when he had attempted to impress a future amorous conquest by taking her to dine at a reputable French restaurant in Ashmeadow.

"I'm afraid we are fully booked this evening," an obnoxious little Gallic man told him at the door.

"I'm sorry, I don't think you understand, I am Colonel Paul Hutchinson," the war hero told him, as he attempted to brush the hindrance aside with a firm hand.

The little Frenchman held on grimly.

"And I am Field Marshal Gaston Lagoutte," he replied. "And even if you were Gerard Depardieu's mother-in-law, you would not have a table here tonight."

Such obstacles are nevertheless rare. After all, Paul Hutchinson had emerged almost unscathed from the Army as well as from two unfortunate marriages. The second Mrs Hutchinson was in a nursing home where patient carers laughed off her incoherent babbling. As far as her predecessor was concerned, she disappeared more than six years ago and her family and the authorities gave up searching almost three years ago.

"She has run away with a Lebanese taxi driver from Coolangatta," he told his fawning entourage with scorn.

They were not sure whether to laugh or not. Was it a joke, or was it the rejection of a humiliation? He did not share with them his concern when the waters of Lake Durrington began to fall dramatically last year. But heavy rain quickly replaced the drought, the waters rose and he was finally relieved to believe that the first Mrs Hutchinson Bligh would continue to rest in a private if muddy peace.

"Women are almost always poor judges of character and adapt badly to a life of rigour and discipline,' he pointed out to his circle of admirers. "If they prefer poverty and boredom living with an uncultivated lout, I will not stand in their way."

"It's very sad, though, to be alone," Elizabeth, a forty-year old spinster told him one morning from one pillow to another.

He laughed. He could see her coming over the horizon like a speeding train.

"Because my unfortunate unions were short-lived, they had a limited effect on my patrimony," he explained. "I enjoy a comfortable retirement, I have a small home overlooking the lake, and I drive a not-very-new Saab convertible that confirms that I am a man of taste and distinction. I am a respected member of several clubs where good manners, inspiring conversations and fine wines go hand in hand."

Elizabeth nodded. She knew he was a member of Rotary and of a small tennis club and believed that that was the extent if his social network. Last night, she had also discovered that he was an incompetent and uninspiring lover. But she preferred to remain silent. She would look elsewhere.

Paul Hutchinson had only one matter of concern, his health. Like most men, he enjoyed an excellent constitution because he did not have the anatomical accessories that cause such discomfort and distress to women throughout their lives. There were, however, occasional moments when twinges, coughs and other discomforts, challenge a man's inner confidence. Such was this morning. The encounter with Elizabeth had depressed him, so he decided to consult Doctor Kofi Smith, just to be assured that he was in perfect male health.

He found himself face-to-face with the one receptionist he always tried to avoid. He had decided a long time ago that she was the type of female that would discourage any man from marriage. She had a loud voice like a sergeant major, she had a moustache like a sergeant major and she barked like a sergeant major that had no respect for rank.

"Can I ask why you are visiting the doctor?" She asked in a voice loud enough to attract the attention of what she thought was her admiring public in the waiting room.

Paul knew very well that she was not supposed to do this but, like most frustrated tyrants, she enjoyed humiliating people. He paused, before answering her question, to ensure that all the other suffering patients were listening. From the corner of his eye, he noted that some patients had lowered their newspaper, hoping desperately that Saint George was about to slay the dragon.

"I was strangling a waitress in a Chinese restaurant last night, when I broke a fingernail," he told her, spacing his words carefully so that all would hear and understand.

She stared at him, opening her mouth two or three times, like a goldfish that has just lost its bowl. The magazine pages had stopped ruffling behind him, and he even heard one or two badly suppressed giggles. Finally, she pointed at the waiting area with a finger, still wondering what to say. As he sat down, near the waiting room door, he noticed that a worried mother had moved her children further down. He had provoked fear, if not respect, which meant nobody would be attempting to drag him into a futile conversation.

He picked up a copy of National Geographic and checked the date. Only twelve years old, this was not bad considering. Opening it on an article discussing the imminent extinction of the blue-tongued frog of Lower Krakapova, he placed it open on the chair, and then sat on it. He noted a few surprised looks.

"I try to avoid the most obvious dangers of a waiting room chair," he explained to the gaping idiots. "It can host to so many illnesses, distresses, leaks, overflows and other emanations. It is very easy to pick up bastard measles, black water fever, anthrax, thrush, herpes or brucellosis by anal penetration, as any officer who has served in the jungle will tell you."

He did not add that his experience of danger had been limited to running a mobile kitchen in the jungle of Aldershot, Hampshire.

Somebody began to giggle and then changed their mind. He faced their inane stares with a penetrating look and they lowered their eyes. He began to inspect his fellow sufferers, because he knew that much can be learned about people by examining their attitude, their dress and their manners, or lack thereof. He decided that the small group in this waiting room was a typical example of the lower rungs of a diversified social ladder.

He chose as an example the middle-aged woman in the left-hand corner, the one who had obviously dyed her hair orange in the laundry sink and who was desperately trying to stay inside a pair of K-Mart jeans at least two sizes too small. He thought that it was reasonably safe to assume that she was divorced and had given up on finding a replacement partner, judging by the blue sweatshirt declaring that all men were bastards and the nicotine stains on her fingers.

"Cholesterol, stress and high blood pressure," he muttered to himself.

In the other corner was a skinny, angry-looking blonde with two kids who both had colds. The boy was about ten and was trying to crack his younger sister's skull open by banging her head against the wall. He decided that the mother was here to ask Kofi for something to calm hyperactivity. She was reading Woman's Day, ignoring their screams and the sour looks from the other patients.

"If I were Kofi Smith," he told himself, "I would prescribe ten strokes each with a leather belt."

He had forgotten for a moment that nowadays it was recommended not to challenge the psychological stability of the little darlings. They were supposed to feel free to express their inner feelings, even if it meant smashing a shelf-load of jam in a local supermarket to relieve stress.

Opposite him sat a little old man. He was thin, pale and quite overwhelmed by the disturbance caused by the little brats. He was gazing at the ground, turning a cloth cap incessantly between gnarled hands. Paul Hutchinson decided that he was here to be told the results of tests, and he had already decided that the news would be bad. He was alone and probably telling himself that there was not really anything worth hanging around for on this planet.

"Ah, well," Paul thought to himself. "Another pensioner's card will soon bite the dust."

Two overweight teenagers sat together. The two girls were holding hands with a look of desperation on their faces, as if prepared to face a disaster of epic proportions. They both wore curtain rings in their nostrils, ears and eyebrows, and both had difficulty in keeping their overflowing buttocks inside their worn jeans. They were both about fifteen, and his decided that the red-head was probably pregnant. He hoped the father was far away on a Liberian cargo ship.

On another chair sat a well-dressed man, with all the characteristics of a middle-class executive. Paul wondered what he was doing here in the middle of the day when most patients are retirees, unemployed or sick children. He was reading the Financial Review.

At that moment, the door to Kofi's surgery opened and a lady emerged holding the hand of a small boy. There was a look of relief on her face so obviously Kofi had been able to reassure her.

"What extraordinary power a doctor holds over simple mortals," he told himself and this was underlined when the doctor called 'Bill!'. The little old man dropped his cap, picked it up with a shaking hand and crept towards the open door looking like a cocker spaniel that has been caught out stealing the cat's dinner. The doctor repeated his call, 'Bill', and the young executive stood up and walked into the surgery, leaving the poor old man to crawl back to his chair on shaking knees.

"I thought he said Phil," he muttered to nobody in particular.

Paul noted with pleasure that he had moved up one slot in the line.

While he mused, a goddess walked into the waiting room. She was around thirty, she was blonde, elegant and beautiful, and he went immediately into cardiac acceleration. She was wearing a lemon coloured two piece suit, a frilly blouse, and the skirt was long enough to be decent and short enough to show that she had admirable legs. As she sat down, with grace and elegance, she caught his eye and smiled.

He smiled back.

"A woman of good taste recognises immediately that in this temple dedicated to depreciated subhuman people, she and I stand out," he decided. "Together we share the love of good taste, fine manners, and the need to be indulgent with those less fortunate than us."

He loved the way she tossed an occasional discreet glance in his direction.

"Was it possible that I had, at last, found the perfect woman, one who would push my past misadventures and irrevocable remedies into the bin of forgotten memories?" he asked himself. "Would she be the one who would teach me that some women can be beautiful, elegant, intelligent and worthy partners for men of my rank and culture?

He tried to avoid her eyes and to resume his study of the renovation of an eighteenth century country house in the Cotswold's.

As he reached the end of the article, he lowered the Country Life magazine he had been using as a flattering screen, and saw that her eyes were still on him. She smiled enticingly.

Suddenly, he realised that this visit had not been in vain.

"This is destiny!" he told himself. "Once out of the surgery, I will wait in the carpark until she emerges, to suggest a quiet lunch together by the lake, a stroll hand-in-hand in the botanical gardens, before showing her my home and my collection of postage stamps commemorating the Battle of Britain. The fact that she is thirty years my junior was unimportant. Age is no barrier when fate throws two people of refined manners into each other's arms. This could well become the great passion, that for which I have waited patiently all my life."

Paul Hutchinson was a renowned strategist, as his supposed activities behind enemy lines in Libya confirmed. By 'great passion', he really meant 'decisive victory'.

He enjoyed the moment. All the ugliness of this room devoted to desperation had disappeared. Two beautiful people had met here, and this chance encounter could probably give birth to a passionate love affair. In years to come somebody might make a film of their story.

"Grace Kelly and William Holden are the kind of actors who could well portray our personalities," he told himself.

He was casting the minor roles in his mind when the door to the surgery opened and the young executive emerged, smiling and shaking Kofi's hand with vigour. The angel rose from her chair.

The patient turned towards her and they ran towards one another in slow motion, as lovers such as Grace Kelly and William Holden used to do.

"It's nothing darling, simply a small hernia," he announced before she threw herself into his arms.

Paul Hutchinson nearly died with humiliation. This overdressed blonde slut had been deliberately teasing him while really waiting for this quite ordinary man who must be her husband or her lover.

Kofi turned towards him.

"Paul, I think it's your turn," he said with a smile.

He stormed angrily past the doctor, muttering angrily, heading for the car park.

"I don't need you," he snapped. "I'm suddenly feeling much, much better."

There was a united gasp of horror as he almost ran out of the building.

He jumped into his car, slamming the door. He watched the loving couple depart in their yellow Stag and drove off in anger.

"Bitch, bitch!" he shouted, thumping the steering wheel with his fist.

Fifteen minutes later he was sitting on his favourite bench, by the lake, gleefully watching the wavelets play over the muddy grave of the first Mrs Hutchinson.

TED, RALPH AND THE MATTRESS

Three hundred and ten people lived in Maverton Plains, a little village about fifty kilometres from the nearest McDonald. In small communities like these, people are very close and share disaster and joys with a stiff upper lip and a six-pack. City people who drove through the village probably asked themselves how anyone would want to live there. There was no simple answer.

In Mavo, as the locals called it, summer was bloody hot, winter was bloody cold and when it rained, the pub offered a free round of drinks. There was not a hill or a clump of trees in view, and the local river, the Dawson, had given up even pretending to be a river more than four years ago. Some reckoned that it got so dusty around Maverton Plains in summer that the sheep had to wear goggles.

Among the good people of the village, Ted Small and Ralph Boss had been mates since childhood, although nowadays their social status had created a small rift. They had gone through a primary school side-by-side where there were only two classrooms. Old Miss Meredith had kept everyone under control with her beady glare and, and Mr Windwalker had puffed and panted his way through thirty-eight asthmatic years of teaching without complaining, even on his deathbed.

"It's so sad," Bill Fisher told Ted Small one evening at the bar when he was feeling in one of his philosophical moods. "An old bloke like that is born, spends his life suffering and then he snuffs it. Twenty years on, nobody even remembers him except for you and me. Is it all worth it, I ask you?"

Ted shook his head and asked for another pint. He was not a philosopher, just a man with a thirst.

Ralph Boss, who owned the Maverton Garage, the Maverton Tow Truck and the Maverton Hardware Store, had the only four-bedroom brick veneer in the town. Behind the house was a big water tank, a gigantic shed and a magnificent swimming pool. In the shed were his treasures, the Range Rover, the Lexus and the Falcon ute, while his wife's Volvo estate wagon sat on the front lawn. Ralph Boss had money and he liked his cars.

At one time he had even owned a small trucking business called 'Maverton Haulage' but it was difficult to manage and he finally came to the conclusion that his drivers were running a business of their own. He sold it to Marcello Sabatini, a wealthy businessman in Melbourne, who needed a small transport business to ensure the distribution of fragile goods.

The Boss Empire did not stop with Ralph. His wife, Mary, owned the only supermarket in town, and his sister, Penny, owned the pharmacy. Ralph's brother, Fred ran the only real estate office. This was why nobody did anything in Maverton Plains without the Boss family knowing about it five minutes before it happened.

The Small family was economically underprivileged. Ted's wife, Alice, worked three days a week stacking the shelves in Mary's supermarket. The way Mary bossed her around, you would never have guessed that they had been good mates at school, sharing everything including boyfriends.

Ted Small, who worked in Ralph Boss's garage as a mechanic, lived with his family in an old weatherboard with a tin roof and a wood burner on Turners Street, There was a Valiant, a Spitfire and a P.76 hidden in the long grass in the back yard, because Ted was a bit of a petrol head. Ralph used to say that Ted couldn't tell the difference between a good car and a lemon, and he was probably right. In Ted's front yard, sat the only working car he owned: a battered Cressida that he parked under the Hills Hoist. Ted's house would have been worth less than a carport in Blaxford.

During their youth, Ralph and Ted had been good friends. It was that time in a boy's life when social ranks had not been an issue. They had both played football for the local team, they had both drank VB, and had both spent some quiet moments on the Mattress with one or two of the more generous local girls.

There were three other brick buildings in Patterson Bend.

The most popular one was the pub, called Fanny's Inn, although she no longer was. It had a saloon bar, a public bar, a bottle shop, a lounge with eight poker machines and a bistro-type restaurant that used to seat eighty people. Ralph Boss drank single malt with his friends from the Lions Club in the saloon bar, Ted Small still preferred his VB but he now drank it in the public bar with his other mates. Nevertheless, some nights when Ted was having problems finding the way home, Ralph would load him in the back of his Range Rover and drop him at his front gate.

The second brick building was the police station. It had an office, a cell, a carport for Brian Spring's Ford Explorer and a small flat out the back. The last time the cell was used was for John Thomas in the autumn of 92. He had rolled in from Alice Springs in a Volkswagen minibus, covered in graffiti and with two girls called Sandy and Mandy with short skirts, heavy make-up and beads in their hair. Nobody knew why he had picked a fight with Fred Atkinson in the pub, but three of Fred's mates had softened him just enough so Brian could put him in the cell for a couple of days to cool down. While he was locked away, the girls had hitched a lift with a passing Maverton Haulage truck and the driver proudly announced a week later that they were now working as 'hostesses' for one of the Sabatini 'clubs' and earning good money.

The third brick building was the Church of Saint Ignatius. It had seen nothing of a religious nature celebrated within its walls since the Vietnam War, but it was the home of the Mattress. This was a large Hessian bag filled with straw about four metres long and two metres wide, and it had been there for many, many years. If the Church had seen no baptisms for a long time, The Mattress had welcomed many unwary virgins and had witnessed several conceptions that had never been immaculate.

Discos, milk bars with jukeboxes or cinemas did not exist in Maverton Plains, so the Mattress became a social launchpad for at least three generations of local teenagers. Bill Fisher reckoned that it was because of the Mattress that the bus that takes the students to the high school in Blaxford carried more and more folded strollers on its roof.

Before they got married, Ralph, Ted, Mary and Alice had often enjoyed a Saturday night together on the Mattress with a couple of bottles of Blue Nun. It was an informal arrangement until the day Mary had announced that she was 'up the duff' and Ralph Boss had proposed to do 'the right thing'. Ted and Alice, feeling lonely on subsequent Saturday nights, decided that they might as well get married too.

Mary Boss gave birth to a daughter, and had no other children. When Stephanie Boss reached the age of fourteen her parents sent her off to a Catholic Boarding School in Melbourne, out of reach of the Mattress. After her VCE, tall blonde and beautiful, she fell passionately in love with Trev, Ted and Alice's Small's only son, three months her junior.

Friendships can become fragile when a wealthy man sees a threat to his grand ambitions for his daughter. One morning, Ralph Boss shouted at his old friend Ted Small, in front of the other mechanics, that he should tell his son to 'keep his dirty hands off my daughter!' Ted was not happy. He remembered how he and Ralph had once played around with other people's daughters in their younger years on the Mattress. But, because he had not had a wage raise in ten years, he kept his thoughts to himself. Jobs were hard to come by in Maverton Plains, especially when your employer and his family owned all the businesses.

The kids went on flirting, although the two mothers tried to keep them apart. Love is love, even in a Godforsaken place like Maverton Plains. Then Ralph Boss fell sick. He went to Melbourne several times, and he looked thinner and greyer every day. The people in the workshop looked at one another and shook their heads, but only when he was not looking. Ralph was a good employer, but he did not like staff shaking their heads during working hours.

One evening he called Ted Small into his office, just as he was leaving. He wanted to take his old friend to Blaxford with him, the next morning. He had an important document to sign at his solicitor's office and wanted Ted to be his witness. When Ralph told him he would have that day off but would still be paid, Ted knew this was serious business.

It was also the first time Ted had had ever travelled in a Lexus. During the drive to Blaxford, Ralph had explained that he wanted Ted to be the witness of his will, because there were things in it of great importance to both of them.

Ian Solin, the solicitor, was bald and he wore gold-rimmed glasses and a pinstriped suit. Ted noticed that his shoes were shiny black and very pointed, not the kind of footwear you would wear around a garage, for sure. He was the senior partner of Solin, McGrane and Cullen and Ted reckoned that he was the kind of solicitor who charged you a thousand dollars just to ask you if the family had enjoyed their holiday on Phillip Island last year.

Ted Small had put on his best jeans, an old but reliable tweed jacket with leather patches on the elbows and a tie commemorating Prince Charles' first marriage. Nevertheless, he still felt ill at ease. It was all oriental rugs, deep leather armchairs, and teak bookcases with leather-bound books and tea in bone china cups. Solin read out the final draft of Ralph Boss's last will and testament, slowly and quietly. Ted Small listened with surprise to the wealth his old friend had gathered, and to the unusual and unexpected dispositions he was taking.

Ralph had lent the money to his sister Penny to buy outright the pharmacy in Maverton Plains, and his death would wipe out any outstanding debts she owed. He left the supermarket, all the cars and the four bedroom brick veneer to his wife. To his daughter, he left a house in Ashmeadow and her grandmother's rings. He left the hardware store to his brother, and ten thousand dollars to each of his mechanics.

Ralph had also instructed that on his death Alice Small, Ted's wife, should receive twenty thousand dollars from his estate so that 'she could get her hair done every week'. Ted remembered that when they were young Ralph used to love running his hands through Alice's long red hair. It brought back old memories: those evenings on the Mattress when Ralph and Alice and Ted and Mary were all good friends.

The biggest surprise was that Ralph had decided to leave the workshop and service station to Ted's son Trev. Like his Dad, Trev was a petrol head, but he had better taste in motor cars. He was currently rebuilding a Jowett Javelin.

Ted signed as the witness without asking any questions. There are matters between old friends that you don't discuss in front of expensive solicitors in pinstriped suits. But when they reached the footpath, he turned toward his mate, mouth open and questions ready to pour out, and was shocked when Ralph grabbed him in his arms and hugged him. He felt two ribs crack. During the drive home, Ralph Boss refused to answer any questions. He simply told his good mate that after his death he would still have a job.

"Unless Trev sacks you, of course," he said with a grin but there were tears in his eyes. "It won't be long, now. The doctor reckons the carburettor will not last more than a few months."

It was a funny way of telling an old mate you were dying of cancer, but country people have their own way of communicating.

"I'm sorry, mate," was about all that Ted Small could say. When you live in Maverton Plains, it's not what you say, it's the way you grab a bloke's arm when you say it.

When Ted got home, he told Alice everything. She cried, wiping her tears on her apron then she got up from the kitchen table, made two mugs of Bushells tea and got some Anzac biscuits out of the tin. Ted remembered Mr Solin's bone china cups and Lady Grey brew and smiled to himself.

Then she began to explain private things, slowly and carefully.

"You've probably noticed that Trev has got a bit of a head for business," she said. "A bit like Ralph."

Ted nodded thoughtfully. "So what?"

She took his hand across the table and squeezed it.

"I never had the courage to tell you but when we got married I was pregnant. Trev is Ralph's son. That's why he's leaving him the garage."

Ted waited a couple of minutes and took a long draft from his mug of tea. Men in the bush do not act like hypersensitive Italians; they digest things slowly and calmly.

"Ah, well. These things happen. We were really good mates, the four of use." was all he could say, after a few minutes of silence and another biscuit.

Alice smiled.

"Really good mates, that's true."

Ted frowned suddenly.

"Wait a bit. That stuffs things up a bit. You and Mary have been talking about Trev and Stephanie and wedding bells, haven't you? Poor kid can't marry his own sister, can he? That's a pity, because I reckon that those two were really made for each other."

Alice smiled.

"It's all right, Ted," she told him softly. "They're not related. Remember, Mary was pregnant when she got married too. You had some good times with Mary on the Mattress."

Ted stared at his wife for a few seconds and then a big grin spread over his face.

"Well, bugger me!" he declared. "I'll be the father of the bride!"

His wife shook her head and waved an admonishing finger at her husband.

"Nobody must ever know," she told him.

The kids got married three weeks before Ralph Boss's death. It was a quiet ceremony attended by everybody in the village, and it was followed by beer and kebabs on the courtyard in front of the garage. They did the same after Ralph's funeral, except there was no bubbly. Maverton was a place where people respected traditions.

When Trev Small took over the garage, he gave his Dad a rise of sixty dollars a week, his first in ten years.

CHARITY BLAKE'S NEW KITCHEN

When Raymond left Charity in 1996 to run away with a female jockey twenty-two years his junior, things became fairly quiet at Charity Blake's brick-veneer in Sutton Vale. Luckily, Charity had kept her home and her job at Globe Providence Insurance. But she had not kept the kids. They were fed up with a mother who spent her weekends with curlers in her hair, a tattered dressing gown on her shoulders, explaining to a half-empty bottle of sherry why all men were bastards. Her daughter, Alice, got a job as an Australian Volunteer in Vanuatu where she fell pregnant to a Methodist preacher from Bolivia, while her sister Karen managed a lesbian night club in country New South Wales with great success. The bland and inane pre-printed poetry expressing love and affection on cheap Christmas cards arrived almost every year.

Charity had two good mates in this big, unfriendly and indifferent world. Shirley Crisp and Maria Cincotta had accompanied her in an indifferent career through high school, and the three friends had experienced marriage and divorce side by side. They all drove twenty year old cars, lived in houses badly in need of renovation and had mortgages they had no hope of paying off. Like true friends, slowly and carefully, Shirley and Maria dragged Charity back into a more positive frame of mind. She threw away the sherry-stained dressing gown, bought an outrageous white mini-dress for her own pleasure, dyed her hair red and declared that she was back on the hunt, with intermittent help from Weight Watchers.

Nowadays, the girls liked to get together on a Friday night for a drink or two, or three, or four, and that Friday night, it was Charity's turn to host the party. Shirley had brought with her a plastic carry bag containing things smelling of Vindaloo and Tandoori as well as a bald and pot-bellied guy she had picked up in the pub. Maria's contribution was a tub of passion fruit ice cream and a can of peaches, and Charity had filled her fridge with two slabs of pre-mixed gin-tonics.

The smell of curry whipped up their appetite and an hour later the fat slob, T-shirt covered in Vindaloo sauce, had fallen asleep on the couch, belly full. As they pulled the tabs on their third round of G & T, listening to him snore, Charity announced exciting news.

"Aunt Susan in New Zealand has kicked the bucket and left me twenty-four thousand dollars. The solicitor says the cheque's in the mail," she declared with a big grin.

There were not going to be any tears for Aunt Susan, that much was obvious. There was a few seconds of deathly silence. Then brains slipped into gear. Suggestions were those of women seeking revenge or wanting to overcome boredom or frustration.

"I'd get myself a new Corolla with that sort of money," Maria declared firmly.

Shirley did not agree.

"That's bullshit," she announced loudly. "Get yourself a facelift. They say that Botox is great for depression."

They all laughed.

Other suggestions fused. A Pacific Island Cruise, three male strippers (one each), a new sofa or a plasma television were given limited consideration.

"Above all, don't waste it on covering the mortgage," Maria said firmly and they all agreed.

"When money drops out of the sky you don't want to be rational," Charity added. "Money has gotta be spent, spending's good for the economy. Ask Kev."

The other girls clapped en enthusiastically. They knew, after listening to months of moaning, that the absolute priority for Charity was a new kitchen.

"You gotta ring up Kitchen Man," Shirley had insisted, finally. "Stainless steel appliances, sexy doors and drawers, solid marble bench tops, a fridge with a TV in the door, you need that, darling. You know something, as Kev used to say? With a new kitchen you might even start cooking again."

Maria did not agree.

"It's got nothing to do with cooking," she had insisted. "It's all about status. All you really need is a good microwave oven and a freezer full of frozen meals. Nobody cooks nowadays, but a sexy kitchen is just as important as a cosy bed."

"You're right!" Shirley had approved. "And it's definitely more useful at her age."

Charity ignored the reference to her advancing years and the ensuing wear and tear. Frequent glances into her rose-tinted mirror encouraged her to believe that she could offer a man a lot of fun under a fluffy duvet, but she was not going to discuss her personal ambitions with Shirley.

In any case, Shirley was a brave girl, and she knew that their good friendship would survive a rude joke. Maria and Shirley also knew that Charity furnished and decorated her house with pride and good taste, and a new kitchen would add to the charm.

The girls all knew about Kitchen Man. You could not switch on the radio or the TV without getting his promotional song. They cracked open another can of G. & T. and began to sing, and even the fat slob on the couch woke up to join in! The song was stolen from Elton John's Rocket Man.

And I think it must have been a long, long time
Cos' that old kitchen's full of cracks and grime
I'm just the man you know you need at home
I will give you laminates and chrome

Oh, yes, Oh yes, I'm Kitchen Man
Kitchen Man, giving you the kitchen of your dreams
Don't forget, cheap copies are never what they seem
Oh Yes, Oh Yes, I'm Kitchen Man,

Before Charity had had time to protest, Shirley had called the 1300 KITCHEN number, and had listened to twenty minutes of Percy Faith's Greatest Hits before getting through to the sales consultant who sounded just like the girl at the Indian take-away. She had assured Shirley that Kitchen Man would be landing on Charity's doorstep, complete with cape and circular saw, the following Tuesday evening, just before 7.30 pm.

Charity usually hated other people trying to run her life, but this time she was secretly rather chuffed. They had enjoyed a few more rounds of drinks while the slob began to snore and then the girls had decided to call it a day, or an early morning as it was.

"Do you want me to leave you that for the night?" Shirley had asked, pointing at the bald gigolo.

Charity had shaken her head.

"We'll stick him in the bus shelter down the road,"Maria decided, grabbing him by the arm. "Who knows, he might strike lucky."

They all laughed.

For Christmas, Shirley had offered Charity a couple of blue movies, hot off the Darwin presses. They were all about lonely housewives calling in horny tradesman. The first one called in a plumber, the second a TV technician. They had both been hot workers and it was with this in mind that Monday evening she slipped into an uplifting piece from B & T and a little black dress from Jacqui E. She had just sprayed herself with a heavy cloud of Eau de Priceline when the front door bell rang *Strangers in the Night*.

Kitchen Man was good-looking, he had a lovely smile, he spoke with a soft voice and he had an impressive catalogue. He measured and sketched and noted. He explained that imitation black marble bench tops were all the rage and that all appliances should have that stainless steel look that proves that the mistress of the house was competent and proficient. Charity flopped on to the couch, remembering a scene from 'Alice and the Horny Plumber', as the hemline of the little black dress crept slowly upwards, displaying enticing thighs. Her visitor was not impressed. He refused to sit down, refused a glass of sherry and a slice of Danish Blue.

Charity decided that Kitchen Man probably preferred the smell of linseed oil to her enticing perfume. He looked like the kind of guy who took the wet clothes out to the Hills Hoist, who emptied the dishwasher and who asked his wife if she would like a cup of tea and a couple of chocolate biscuits while he cleaned the oven.

She sighed in despair, pulled down her skirt and decided that her visitor was boring, domesticated and faithful to the hilt. Without even casting a glance at her cleavage, he departed, promising a quote within three days.

Nine thousand dollars seemed quite reasonable to Charity before she realized that this did not include the appliances, the new floor, the new sink and the tiles behind the new sink. Nevertheless, she signed, gave him a deposit and went out to buy the best domestic appliances that Europe and Great Mates in Blaxford had to offer. Her cousin George had been working there for fifteen years, so she knew she would be well advised and not cheated. Work had begun three weeks later, at seven in the morning.

When she got back from work that first evening, she sat down on her couch to cry. The kitchen looked as if it had been visited by an Iraqi suicide bomber and the old wall oven was lying on its side in the front garden beside the letterbox. The carport was full of cracked doors, bashed drawers, pieces of broken wood and nails. She had eaten a take-away pizza and had watched Master Chef on her new plasma screen coated in a thick layer of old kitchen dust. It was probably the wrong choice of programme, she muttered to herself as she gave up and went to bed.

One week and ten centimetres of dust later, she learned that the cabinet maker was closed for the summer holidays and that the container which contained the wall oven, the cook top and the microwave ordered from Good Mates had been swept off the deck of the *Lucrecia Borgia* by a freak wave. Kitchen Man had told her not to fret, because she had forgotten to sign the acceptance of the quotes submitted by his friends, the electrician and the plumber. Their work was going to be slightly delayed as Volt Man was attending a Christian Revival Seminar in Tonga and Tap Man was having a new nose fitted in a hospital in Shanghai. Meanwhile, she had signed away a further twelve hundred dollars and her hand had been shaking so much that Kitchen Man had had to guide the pen across the cheque.

Two weeks later, the whole team was at work, nearly. Kitchen Man would leave now and again for a couple of days as he started work on other kitchen projects. Tap Man would cut and bend pipes in her front garden listening to hard rock on a black and yellow transistor radio slightly smaller than a Mini. The neighbours complained every day. Volt Man ripped out all the old light and power fittings and left wires hanging everywhere while he went away to finish a job in Tasmania.

By this time, Charity had been without a kitchen for five weeks. She rang cousin George at Good Mates who told her not to worry. Her project was looking good, he assured her.

The guys from *Domino Pizza, Pizza Hut, Noodle Box, the Golden Dragon Take-Away, Bengali Delites* and *Nippon Sushi* knew her address by heart. Most evenings she would eat sitting in the old Nissan Bluebird in the car port because looking at the ruins of her kitchen and family room depressed her. Late one night SBS showed a documentary film about the London Blitz, and it made her almost feel at home.

She had taken a fortnight off from work, hoping that if she was in the house all day glaring she might frighten them into accelerated action. It hadn't worked. She had discovered that during the day she had to leave her car in the street, because Kitchen Man's van was in her carport, Tap Man's Ute was in the driveway, and Volt Man's truck was on her front lawn. Strangers were wandering over her flowerbeds rummaging through the rubble and derelict appliances, one of them even had a metal detector! The dust was now so thick that when she opened the front door it set up an opaque storm.

One evening she had come home with the shopping and found Kitchen Man, Volt Man and Tap Man settled on her couch cooking a spaghetti marinara on a camper stove and watching TV on her plasma TV. She rang Maria who took her out for a Tandoori and she ate slowly with tears of desperation running down her face.

The next day, she took a decision. She called the three tradesmen together and announced that if all was not finished within the next fortnight, she would be taking drastic action. As she spoke, she ran the blade of a large carving knife across her thumb as if to test its sharpness. Volt Man laughed but Tap Man disappeared under the sink and began tightening something desperately.

"Don't be silly," Kitchen Man protested mildly with a smile.

Charity took a short step towards him, knife raised.

"You'll be the first," she warned coldly. "The others will watch."

She rang Shirley the next morning to tell her about the threat.

"Shit!" was all her friend could find as a comment.

But the message had been received loud and clear. When all the pipes stopped leaking and the lights began to work, she knew that there was still hope. Cousin George personally delivered Daipong appliances to replace the European products lost at sea and the cabinetmakers came back from a seminar in Thailand to finish the bench tops, doors and drawers. When she heard the black pseudo-marble tops fall into place with a heavy 'clunk', she sat on the floor and sobbed with relief.

The handles she had wanted were out of stock so she accepted a more expensive model, but at a discount. The doors were also dearer because the factory had misread the order and prepared a deluxe model favoured by the Duchess of Bogliano. She accepted to pay an extra three hundred dollars more than the five hundred quoted. During negotiations, the carving knife never left her hand. When Kitchen Man finally slipped the Daipong dishwasher into its cavity, Charity realised that she was approaching the end of her martyrdom.

Kitchen Man looked quite relieved to leave and told her, unconvincingly, how much he had enjoyed the job. He even took a few photos before he left to show future clients what a success it had been. In one of the photos, she still had the carving knife in her hand.

She called in an industrial cleaning firm that turned up with a giant vacuum cleaner to suck away all the dust. Slowly the plasma screen had taken on its old sparkle and the beige couch had given way to the good old chocolate couch she had always loved. Her lovely house was reborn.

Shirley and Maria came round on the following Friday to admire her new asset.

"With a kitchen like that, you could get yourself a new bloke," Shirley suggested.

"You must have some money left over," Maria proposed. "You could get some decking out the back with a three-seater spa."

Charity tried to imagine guys digging up her flowerbeds, tearing out the lawn, hacking the branches off her apple and lemon trees, chopping down her roses. She shuddered.

"No thanks," she said.

Shirley suggested that the three girls could have cooked dinner together that evening.

"Are you crazy? We're not dirtying my new kitchen," Charity said. "No bloody way! We'll get a take-away!"

THE PERFECT CRIME

Nobody in Ashmeadow would have guessed that Ken Moorhouse was an unhappy man. Nobody would have believed that while he sold fine jewellery and beautiful time pieces in a magnificent shop passed down from generation after generation of jewellers, he was not satisfied with his profession. Nobody would have suspected that Ken dreamed of sitting in the dunes with easel, canvas and paintbrushes, far, far away from the stifling atmosphere of the old jewellery shop.

The little town of Ashmeadow used to be a haven of serenity. It sat in the Northern stretches of the Peninsula, far from rumbling trains and roaring motorways, and there was neither airport nor stadium within fifty kilometres. It was a region that wheelers, dealers, politicians and real estate developers had overlooked.

During the last federal election, only one candidate had led a campaign in the forgotten town and the surrounding countryside: Alice Button had represented the people of Ashmeadow for eighteen years as an independent, and the professional politicians on both sides of the divide had decided to let her be. She was also the granddaughter and daughter of the two previous mayors.

People in Ashmeadow enjoyed tradition and stability.

The town was the commercial hub for the small communities living at the top of the peninsula. It was a market town, selling local produce such as olive oil, almonds, mushrooms, trout, potatoes and a very pungent blue goats milk cheese, known in the region as Blue Thunder, because of the embarrassing effects it could have on the digestive system of certain consumers.

It had a small supermarket, a hardware store, a drapery, a butchery, a pub, a police station, a French restaurant, a bookshop and a magnificent jewellers shop. There was a farmers' market every Saturday on the square in front of the town hall, and not only would the locals sell their produce but traders from around the region would come to offer jeans, shirts, microwave ovens and plastic sandals made in China.

The town even boasted its own herbal therapist. In a small flat over the butchery lived Lucienne Bois, a generous soul who offered miracle remedies and comforting words to her visitors. Most of them were lonely men, those who had never married or those who had somehow lost their wives due to good or bad fortune. If her visitors sometimes left her premises with flushed cheeks and a twinkle in the eye, it was of no concern to the township. The people of Ashmeadow did not encourage malicious gossip.

Of course, things had changed, gradually and painfully, due to external influences. Progress had brought motor cars, telephones, refrigerators, transistor radios, television and other paraphernalia. The supermarket even offered packaged food that became haute *cuisine* after only four minutes in a microwave oven.

Nevertheless, some traditions were set in stone and in the middle of the modern technological revolution sat Ken Moorhouse in his magnificent and very traditional jewellers shop. He was the son, grandson and great-grandson of the only jewellers of Ashmeadow, and customers, called 'patrons', came from all across Victoria. The black-wood display counters and cabinets in his shop had been there for four generations, and the shoes of nearly one hundred years of satisfied customers had scraped and polished the wooden floors.

Ken Moorhouse did not sell products from Taiwan or Romania. His clocks and watches came from France or Switzerland, his fine *objets d'art* come from local and foreign artisans of good repute and his best jewellery was made in the shop itself, from gold, silver and semi-precious and precious stones. The Moorhouse family had made the rings, brooches and necklaces worn by some of Victoria's finest ladies, and kept records of them all. The police knew of his ledgers and his skills, and the archives held by generations of the family had helped bring many thieves and burglars to justice.

His wares were so fine that rumourmongers claimed that Marcello Sabatini, head of the largest crime syndicate in Melbourne, actually bought presents there for his wife and his mistresses and had placed the business under his personal but discreet protection. The business employed competent staff. Miss Harris and Mrs Stickler managed the front counter with patience and courtesy. Frank Lucas was an excellent watchmaker and Jeff Whitley had been making and repairing fine jewellery for the family for more than thirty years.

Ken Moorhouse sat in a little back office and only emerged when the bell over the shop door announced a visitor. Then he would appear, smiling and offering the visitor gracious and flattering compliments. When his customer had spent enough money, he would rush out from behind the counter, open the shop door, bow, smile, and assure the caller that their visit had caused him great pleasure as well as an immense honour. They were the words his father and grandfather had used before him. He was faithful to the tradition, but without pleasure. Sadly, while the village jeweller was rich, he had neither wife nor mistress to favour, nor children to spoil, and there was much unspoken speculation as to what would happen to the business after his death.

At midday, he would eat, always alone, at *Chez Victor*, the town's restaurant, his lunch always accompanied by a glass of white wine. Sometimes, on a Friday evening, he would back the old Humber Snipe out of the garage and drive to Melbourne for the weekend, to visit friends or to enjoy the latest exhibitions or shows.

Ken loved the Saturday morning market, which he visited regularly. Every week he would buy a few bottles of local wine, a slice of the local cheese, some smoked ham, some fresh tomatoes and a couple of pork chops. Sometimes he found a watercolour or an old piece of pottery. On the eighteenth of October, he discovered Angelique.

She was serving on a stand offering fresh vegetables, and when he saw her, he knew that the gods had placed her on his path. Angelique was very beautiful. She was not more than twenty-five years of age, with raven black hair that shimmered in the sun, a skin like wild honey and bright blue eyes. As she moved around the stand, serving her customers, she chatted, smiled and spread happiness around her. He loved the way her long floral skirt flowed around her full hips, and he saw that her peasant blouse contained great promises. At the age of forty-three, Ken had a very limited knowledge and understanding of women, but it seemed to him that here was beauty and purity of a quality rarely seen in Ashmeadow.

It began with discreet lunches, then candle-lit diners and later hand-clutching visits to the cinema, always in the nearby city of Blaxford, to avoid prying eyes and indiscreet questions. Despite these precautions, and after a few weeks of secret meetings, the poor man realized that he could no longer spend any more of those long lonely days in his boring and bleak office. He needed Angelique by his side.

On the eleventh of December, he blushingly presented his new trainee secretary to his astonished staff.

Angelique was a most unusual secretary. She never answered the phone, she never typed a letter and she had the annoying habit of sticking her tongue out at Mrs Stickler when she entered the office. She spent much of her time painting her toenails, glossing her lips or telling her employer amusing stories about her life as a young girl in a village near the Mediterranean Sea. Visitors to the shop were often very surprised by the peals of laughter coming from what was usually a formal and bleak office.

After a few weeks, and particularly after the New Year Sales, Angelique realized that her darling Ken was not a happy man. She questioned him gently, little by little, day by day, and discovered that he no longer wanted to spend his days in the dark back office of a small jewellers shop in a small country town. He wanted to climb the Rockies, to sail the Mediterranean, to eat Lacquered Duck in Hong Kong, to play petanque with Vanessa Paradis or to watch female mud-wrestling in Manchester City. More importantly, he wanted to do all of this with *la belle Angelique* at his side.

There was no simple solution. He could not sell the business, nor could he withdraw too much money. Each Moorhouse had promised his father on his deathbed that he would maintain and enhance the family business. However, as everyone knows, to every problem, there is a solution, and the wonderful Angelique found the answer.

"We will rob the shop!" she declared one evening over a quiet dinner. "All that fine jewellery, those precious stones and those magnificent watches in your safes, what would they be worth?"

"About two million dollars," Ken admitted, thoughtfully munching an asparagus tip. Before realising the enormity of what she had suggested. "But we can't do that. It would be a burglary, a terrible crime!"

She laughed wickedly at him across the table.

"How can it be a crime if you are stealing from yourself?" she asked pertinently. "You will be taking what belongs to you, my darling."

Ken Moorhouse thought for a few seconds of all the happiness he could buy from such an illogical act. He decided that it was time to be courageous, irrational, ambitious and fearless. He had been 'reasonable' for too long. With Angelique at his side, he would dare!

"Of course, you are insured," she added. "That insurance company must have made a fortune from your family over the generations."

Ken nodded.

"That's true," he murmured thoughtfully. "Of course, if there was a burglary, Mrs Stickers would put in a claim immediately, without knowing that it was I who had taken the stock".

She clapped her hands in glee.

"Well, I can hardly imagine that you would tell your staff that you were going to burgle your own shop, would you?"

He agreed reluctantly that she was probably right.

Angelique arranged the burglary for the following Monday evening because Monday evenings were always very quiet in Ashmeadow. Ahmed, who ran the market stall where Angelique had been working when she and Ken first met, would drive the getaway van.

Ken Moorhouse opened the three safes at nine thirty that evening. In less than forty minutes, he and Angelique had moved all the boxes into the waiting van, deliberately damaging some of the showcases and display cabinets. While Angelique climbed into the van next to Ahmed, illogically, the jeweller went back inside the shop to lock up.

Ten minutes later, when the jeweller reached the footpath, closing the shop door furtively behind himself, the van, the stock and beautiful Angelique had disappeared.

He thought about it all very carefully, for nearly an hour, sitting in his dingy back office, sipping a chamomile. Finally, and with a deep sigh, he decided to call his old friend Peter Masters at the police station. The policeman wrote down everything Ken Moorhouse told him in a large notebook and then told him what had happened, as seen by an officer of the law.

"You see, there was no burglary," he explained, stroking his moustache with a nonchalant finger. "You opened your shop and your safe and gave the goods yourself to Mr and Mrs Mahmud."

Ken frowned.

"Mr and Mrs Mahmud?"

His friend patted his hand gently.

"Yes, your secretary was the wife of Ahmed, the man who ran the vegetable stall at the market."

Ken's heart fell into a bottomless pit. His dream of freedom and happiness had endangered the business his father had passed down to him. He was ashamed.

"And because you gave them the jewellery and the precious stones, there is no burglary. And if there is no burglary, there is no crime and no insurance", the policeman explained. "All you have done is to offer a magnificent gift to the lovely couple. You're insured with Global Providence Insurance, aren't you?"

The jeweller nodded glumly.

"I would avoid putting in a claim, if I were you," the friendly policeman advised him.

The poor jeweller was devastated. He realised that he would soon be the laughing stock of the village. He sighed, thinking of the work ahead of him, the efforts required to restore confidence and to renew his image as a competent and unimaginative businessman.

"Unless you want to report a crime and ask me to arrest you?" Peter Masters suggested gently.

The sad little jeweller shook his head.

"I'm sure they will be very happy, "added the policeman.

Peter Masters did receive a call from the Sabatini family when news of the crime hit Melbourne. They assured him that the jewels could be collected and that relatives of Marcello could ensure an eternal holiday for the Mahmud couple at the bottom of a little bay in Sicily, with no embarrassing questions to be answered. He told them that Ken Moorhouse was not that kind of man. He added that they should only call him on his private line, not in the office. People talk.

Ken cried when he received the photos from Venice. He had always wanted to travel, and somehow he felt suddenly reassured that his jewellery had been put to good use. The very pregnant Angelique looked delightfully happy in her gondola. The ring on her finger had been one of his most prestigious pieces.

His thoughts were interrupted by the doorbell announcing the arrival of a customer. He hid the happy photograph in the drawer of his desk, stood up, took a deep breath, straightened his back and strode towards the shop and a life of monotony.

"Mrs Featherby," he exclaimed, bowing and smiling. "What an honour and pleasure to see you. How can we help you today?"

BERNADETTE FALLS IN LOVE

"I have never hitch-hiked before," the woman explained nervously.

"It's O.K., I enjoy the company and you're perfectly safe with me," he replied.

Taking one hand off the steering wheel he extended it to his passenger. She shook the extended hand very formally.

"Tony," he said.

"Bernadette," she replied.

He was driving slowly because the road was narrow and winding, and another vehicle could be hiding behind every hill or corner. He was driving slowly because he had more than a hundred dozen fresh farm eggs in the back of the van, and he did not want any complaints about breakage. He was driving slowly because he could feel that this young woman wanted to talk. Sometimes, it is easier to talk of private, secret things, to a stranger.

"You came from France?" he asked, having recognised her accent.

She nodded, gazing wistfully through the windscreen. This part of Victoria had almost a European feel about it, and she could well imagine herself travelling on a French country road, and she felt as if a billboard for Vittel mineral water or a famous brand of Camembert could appear at any moment.

"France was not really my country," she explained. "My parents were residents of Algeria and we had to leave in the middle of that dreadful civil war".

"The war of independence," Tony commented. "You called it an uprising but it was really a war for independence."

Bernadette sighed.

"We did not understand at that time. It was a colonial era, we thought that they needed our guidance and care. Later, I read about the brutality, the torture, it was terrible."

"Then de Gaulle gave them their independence by organising a referendum where the French settlers were not allowed to vote," the driver concluded. "This was the man they elected as President because they thought he would defend the Empire."

Bernadette was startled.

"How do you know all this?" she asked, frowning.

She felt that her past was private; her history was not to be touched by others.

The elderly man smiled gently.

"I was a journalist working for a British newspaper in North Africa at that time. I, too, am a migrant."

She nodded.

"We'll be in Blaxford in about ten minutes,"the driver announced. "Do you live there?"

She smiled wistfully.

"My parents settled here, and they set up a business, designing and making wedding dresses. Within five years, we had eleven employees and *Vendome* bridal gowns were selling as far away as Brisbane and Adelaide."

Tony laughed. She suddenly discovered that despite his age he was quite handsome when he laughed.

"It's a small world. Would you believe that my daughter was married in Midvale in 1968 wearing a *Vendome* gown? Your mother is a very good designer."

"I no longer have a mother, and there no longer is a business," Bernadette replied sadly. "My parents went to France on holiday last year and were killed in a car accident. I have come today from the solicitor. There were debts and the company was placed into liquidation. I go back to Blaxford to find myself a job and maybe a husband."

The driver cast a discreet glance in her direction. She must be in her late twenties, and she was not a particularly pretty girl. He thought that the hunt for a partner might not be an easy task.

"I worked in my mother's factory, I am a good seamstress, so I might find work," she said softly, almost defiantly, as she felt the man's gaze upon her. "There is a man who has asked me to marry him, twice already."

"Then all is well," concluded the driver, casting a discreet glance at her shabby, worn shoes and remembering the small cardboard suitcase in the back of the van.

"He is twenty years older than me," she said sadly. "He is very rich."

He did not reply. They came round a final bend and the town appeared before them. The driver imagined a man who perhaps saw her as a live-in cook, a housemaid as well as a wench to keep his bed warm in winter.

Unwittingly, he had read Victor Maddock's mind perfectly. When he helped her out of the van he gave her a business card.

"Just in case you need a few dozen eggs for the wedding," he said with a gentle smile.

Four months later she called him on the phone.

"I am getting married next month," she announced with no excitement in her voice. "Would you come as my only guest?"

He hesitated only slightly.

"I would love to. But why your 'only guest?'"

"I have no friends or relatives," she explained. "All the other guests are relatives or friends of my husband-to-be."

Tony felt a sudden weight of sadness, like a stone in his heart.

"I would be proud if I was invited as your good friend," he suggested. "Very proud."

She laughed.

"Then we will do it better. You will be my best friend, Tony. I will tell Victor."

"Victor?"

"My future husband, Victor Maddock."

Tony hung up slowly. He had met Victor Maddock a couple of times, and had heard much about him. He was known as a mean man, reluctant to pay a compliment or a bill for that matter. He drove a large vintage Jaguar, and gentlemen raised their hats when they met him in the streets. He owned five buildings in the main street of Ashmeadow, which he rented to local shop owners. He was one of these gentlemen of whom some people speak in awe because they seem to make money without ever perspiring.

The wedding was celebrated in Ashmeadow, and was a sad affair. Victor had appointed two young girls from the village to act as bridesmaids, and a friend from Blaxford was his best man. For the lunch, he had ordered the fixed daily menu in a local pub and a cheap bubbly wine to toast the bride. The barman whispered that the groom wore a suit inherited from his dead father and had ordered three matching floral dresses from *Burdine*'s for the bride and the two bridesmaids. It was probably true. Bernadette cast several worried looks in Tony's direction during the festivities, and he beamed back encouragingly with the widest smile he could muster.

He invited her to dance, and she accepted with joy. Tony loved the waltz and was delighted with the fairy-like lightness and grace of his partner.

"Your husband is glaring at me," he whispered in her ear. "I think he is jealous. You are looking very beautiful today."

Tony received a postcard from Bernadette three days later. For their honeymoon, Victor had taken her to a bed and breakfast in Sutton Vale. Every day, he fished by the lake while she read the paperback love stories he had bought second-hand in the local market near the lake.

When Tony made his deliveries in the village where Victor and Bernadette lived, he heard occasional comments about the marriage.

"Better than poverty and solitude for her, I suppose," said Fred from the Café Bellevue.

Jonathan, the butcher, was less indulgent.

"Better than paying the services of a whore once a week," he said spitefully. "Probably cheaper, he gets a cook and a housemaid thrown in for the same price."

James Turnbull, from the local supermarket, considered Victor almost a friend. He told Tony that he was a careful municipal councillor, a boring philatelist, an inconspicuous member of the National Party, and a prudent card player.

After the honeymoon, Victor set about finding his wife a job. He told friends, the few he had, that she needed to feel that she was making a contribution to her upkeep. It was not a simple matter, he explained, as she had no formal qualifications, but several reluctant offers for employment appeared. They came from people who did not like him but who respected his money and his status.

The final list of proposed jobs was short and simple: she could work in a local pastry shop, do ironing for the mayor's wife or be employed as a cleaner in the Blaxford Hospital. Victor decided that she would take up a job in the hospital, because, he told her, he would be proud to see her serving the community. The truth was that he preferred to see her far away, sheltered from the comments his neighbours may have made if they had seen his wife employed in a menial role in his own village.

The hospital's administrator, Bill Weatherby, a political animal and ally of Victor in some fields, was reluctant.

"People will ask me why I offer a job to the wife of a wealthy man when there were so many underprivileged women looking for work," he suggested.

"She will work under her maiden name," Victor decided, brushing aside the minor obstacle with a sweeping gesture. "Besides, who is going to stare at a woman in a blue uniform pushing mop and bucket in the gloomy corridors of your old hospital?"

Bill nodded reluctantly.

"We will be looking at budget estimates in three months,"Victor reminded him. "I have friends well placed."

Bill nodded enthusiastically. Bernadette would start on the 3rd of March.

There was no regular bus service into town, so Victor generously offered her a second hand Vespa. She discovered that car drivers were the most selfish and arrogant members of the community. She had to cover a few kilometres on the main road, always heavy with cars and trucks. In summer, it was still daylight when she rode home, but in winter, each trip was a fearful experience. On the main road, she would feel the headlights on her back all the way, and she prayed that each driver would see her frail black silhouette perched above a weak little red tail light. On rainy nights, they sprayed her with water and mud as they swept past. The last stretch was on a winding country road through the hills, where drivers had the habit of cutting corners at high speed. Each dip would be filled with clammy patches of fog, and several times, she was forced into a wet ditch by a driver oblivious of her very existence.

Her husband sat in the local pub waiting impatiently for her to arrive. Occasionally, he sat with the girl, and money exchanged hands. When Bernadette would push open the door to announce her arrival, the girl would have already left and Victor would quickly empty his glass, bid farewell to his friends, and come to the door to greet her.

"You mustn't come in here," he told her, the first time, offering a forced smile between clenched teeth. "Only women of bad repute come into bars. Anyhow, you're covered in mud."

After a few too many beers, one night, Fred spoke up, after too many beers.

"You're a bastard, Victor Maddock," he slurred. "You won't let your wife sit next to the fire in the public bar when she arrives wet and muddy, because only sluts come in bars, so you say. Well, what about the girl, she comes in two or three times a week, and you don't seem to mind?"

"It's my business, and I'll ask you to mind yours!" Victor shouted angrily.

Bernadette accepted meekly her fate. She did not care to remind him that several of his friends would take their wives to the pub in the evening. The women would chat over a glass of wine or a shandy while the men played darts or pool and shared jokes. But not Bernadette.

Victor and Bernadette would go home; he would sit himself in front of the television to watch the news or a game show, while she withdrew to the kitchen to prepare his evening meal. They went to bed every night a ten o'clock sharp.

The weekends were devoted to gardening, going to a local football or cricket match and, even a visit to the cinema complex in Blaxford. They settled into the monotony of a sedate, unimaginative life of marriage, although the seeds of mutual affection appeared gradually. There were moments when he clasped her hand in the safe darkness of the cinema.

"You are a beautiful woman," he told her, one Sunday, over a pepperoni pizza.

He knew that he would have to talk to her about the girl, but he was not yet ready. He needed the confidence that a strong, mutual respect could bring.

They took four weeks holiday every year, in August, and every holiday was the same: visiting his aunt in Luxton Valley. They would pick mushrooms, take long walks, holding hands now almost every time, and, together, do odd jobs around the old lady's house. Bernadette and Aunt Maud became good friends, confidants, and Victor discovered that there were moments when he was almost proud of his wife.

"She is a good woman," Aunt Maud told him one day. "You don't deserve her. You will have to tell her about the girl, one day, you know. She'll understand."

Occasionally,Tony would pass by the house on a Saturday morning, proposing a box of freshly-laid eggs as a gift.

"What have you done to the man?" he whispered to her during one of his visits." He greeted me with a smile this morning and offered me a bottle of wine from his personal reserve!"

Bernadette shook her head.

"I don't know. He treats me well; he has become kinder and more caring over recent months."

"Perhaps he's in love?" Tony suggested with a grin. "Lucky bastard!"

For their tenth wedding anniversary, Victor bought her a fine dress and took her out to dinner at a fine hotel in Blaxford, and, on the spur of the moment, they spent the night in one of the hotels' famous four poster beds. When he strolled through the village with his wife on his arm, he smiled, sometimes greeting an acquaintance with a joyful quip. The shopkeepers, baffled by this change of spirit, looked at one another and shook their heads.

Five days before their fifteenth wedding anniversary, Aunt Maud died, peacefully, in her sleep. Bernadette would never have suspected her husband of being emotive, and his weeping shocked her. She took him in her arms, and they hugged one another with passion. Between sobs, he told here that his aunt had said marrying her had been the best decision the old fool had ever made in his life. He then grabbed her by the shoulders, looked deep into her eyes, and told her that he loved her.

They spent several weeks in the magnificent country house he had inherited from his aunt, cleaning out more than ninety years of futile memories. He put the house up for sale and was not surprised when a couple from Hong Kong, recent migrants, appeared, exchanging excited cries in Mandarin.

"This is the new Australia", he told her glumly, when they left. "We are no longer an island but a cauldron of conflicting cultures. They will pay dearly for a slice of my country."

He asked for an exorbitant price and when the agent rang to say they had accepted, she saw Victor laugh for the first time, with unrestrained glee. He grabbed her by the hand, dragged her upstairs, and made love to her with unrestrained passion.

Once he had caught his breath, he announced that his aunt had left instructions. The money he had inherited was to be devoted to his wife, and he would respect her last wishes. The following Friday, he took her to the local Peugeot dealer and bought her a new car. It was bright red, a French beauty, like her, so he said. Never before in her life had she been described as beautiful.

The following summer was the biggest shock of all. As they no longer had an old lady to host their holidays he took her to France, the birthplace of her parents, for a tardy honeymoon. They visited Paris, Cannes and a ski resort in the Alps. He laughed with delight when he saw a ski instructor in Chamonix flirting with her.

"He's after your money," he told her, and then roared with laughter. "Unless you are more beautiful than you think. Has he, like me, discovered your hidden charms?"

He tried, desperately, to speak a little French to please her, and was delighted to see that her own memories of the language had been only dormant. She could not believe that this gay, loving man was the cold miser she had married so long ago. There was only one last hurdle to overcome. Soon, very soon, he would have to talk about the girl.

Back home, the following winter was so different! She had insisted on keeping her job but now she would come home from work in a warm, comfortable car. She would park her little Peugeot in front of the pub and join him and his friends for a glass of wine. He would throw his arms around her to hug her when she entered the bar and she loved this public demonstration of affection.

"You have driven him mad with passion," one of his friends whispered in her ear. "When you inherit his money, give me a call."

Others murmured to each about the girl, and how she always left the pub about an hour before Bernadette arrived. Why the silly old fool was philandering with a girl in her early twenties was not only inexplicable, but also inadmissible. Bernadette ignored the potential threat to her happiness. She explored her mother's old cookbooks, preparing for him the most delightful recipes she could discover. He delighted in her culinary skills, and often invited friends home on a Saturday night to taste the fine menu prepared by 'Victoria's famous French chef'!

Then, one evening, in the pub, he doubled up, gasped in pain and vomited his drink over the table. It was the first time that she saw her husband flushed with shame. As she drove him home, he told her that he had been suffering from acute stomach pains for several months, and was due to see Kofi the next day to discuss the X-rays he had undergone secretly three weeks before. Within a week, they knew that he had a malignant tumour in his stomach.

When he heard how much the operation would cost, how futile it would be and how much torture he would have to suffer, he announced that he would go home to bed, take morphine prescribed by the doctor, and await the fate the Creator had in store for him, his darling wife by his side. She left her job immediately and devoted the next eighty-four days to his care.

He prepared his death with dignity. He asked the director of the funeral parlour to come and take his orders. He was to be cremated, and he negotiated a price that was based on a macabre deal: he wanted his body wrapped in a sheet and placed in a pine wood coffin.

"I have something to tell you," he whispered one morning. "It's about a girl."

He never found the strength or the courage to fulfil his promise.

Kofi had given him a generous prescription of painkillers, and she noticed that he was taking them more and more frequently. He was thin, pale, exhausted. Ted Farmington, the local vet and one of Victor's oldest friends, came to visit Victor one day, and she was shut out of the room during their meeting. Their discussion was lively, but as they whispered or hissed their verbal exchanges, she could not hear or understand what was happening. Finally, the vet left, red in the face and told her that he would be coming back next Thursday and to have everything ready.

She thought that he wanted her to bake the chocolate cake he loved.

Ted Farmington arrived at three o'clock, and she had prepared coffee and the chocolate cake, although her poor Victor could not eat. The vet looked very solemn as he took off his coat, and the men were quiet while she served the coffee in Victor's bedroom. She noticed that they were holding hands, as old friends might do when the moment is grave. Then Victor kissed her and asked her to leave the room. They had to discuss 'men's business'. Ted left about an hour later, on tiptoes, closing the door quietly behind him.

"He's asleep," he told her. "Better let him rest a while."

When she went to see him an hour later, he was smiling and dead. It was the 7th of July, and the village was wrapped in fog. She rang Kofi who came over and signed the death certificate with a whimsical look.

"Give my regards to Ted," he told her. "I suppose that I'll see him at the funeral."

She was surprised to see the number of people who attended her husband's memorial service. She did not know him to have so many friends. She was surprised to see a young woman, quite pretty, but overcome with grief.

Her good and faithful friend was there, at her side, and saw the regards she threw in the girl's direction.

"That's Victor's girl," he whispered. "Everybody talks about her but nobody knows who she is."

Because she was his only heir, formalities were relatively simple. She inherited seven buildings, two bank accounts containing more than two million dollars and a collection of oil paintings in a bank vault in Melbourne. There was also a letter from Victor. He asked her to continue to pay the monthly allocation he had granted to a young lady in Blaxford called Betty Martin, who was his natural daughter.

Betty was the girl, and she had been brought up by foster parents because her young mother died when giving birth. Bernadette discovered the weekly transfers that must have been going on for years. She also found the girl's address. She decided that Betty would be the daughter she had not been able to offer to Victor.

Betty and Bernadette soon became good friends, and talked about the wonderful, generous Victor every time they met. When Bernadette opened her restaurant in Ashmeadow, Betty joined her in the kitchen and has since become her partner in business.

The restaurant is called '*Chez Victor*' a tribute to the man they still love and remember with deep affection.

FRANK BLISS, CONSULTANT EXTRAORDINAIRE

Gerard first met Frank during a lunch break at a large seminar in Melbourne. Suddenly, across a crowded room, he saw somebody who looked totally out of place, even more so than himself. As the attendance at the seminar was not by invitation but an open house event, there were several struggling small-time consultants attending, hoping to find out what the big, beautiful and internationally successful enemy was planning. They were also there to enjoy their favourite commodity: free food and drink. For Gerard, it was obvious that the poor man was one of them.

He was an aspiring consultant himself. He had come to Melbourne from Adelaide, having fallen in love with a local paediatrician. Her friends rumoured that his 'love' had been inspired by practical factors such as her comfortable home, respectable income and a car twice as big as his. According to their spiteful gossip, he had abandoned belongings of little value: an old ginger cat, a pokey flat in Glenelg and his membership of the Port Adelaide Football Club. He ignored their malicious comments, determined to show that even people from Adelaide can succeed in the big, bright and aggressive city of Melbourne.

The stranger Gerard saw today had that despairing look that he knew so well and had seen in the eyes of many people who had lost a long-term job and believed that their acquired experience could justify them calling themselves a 'consultant'. As a cynical friend of his once said, when times are tough, consultants crawl out from under the carpets like cockroaches. He smiled encouragingly at the lost soul, and the lost soul looked surprised for a moment before smiling back. Gerard fought his way across the crowd towards him and they shook sweaty hands.

"Gerard Bigglesmith, business consultant," he announced.

"Frank Bliss, strategic advisor," the stranger replied.

"Great seminar," Gerard suggested.

Frank nodded.

This magnificent event had been organised by the Melbourne office of Wistfull Harmless and Grabbett, international consultants. These experts, with offices in Singapore, Kuala Lumpur and Tokyo, hoped to persuade ambitious executives to use their expensive but shrewd business planning services.As many know,a career as a successful strategic management consultant is far, far better than spending a lifetime picking raspberries in Daylesford. They announced that big was beautiful, that ambition was indispensable, that charity began with a bank deposit in Switzerland and that with Wistfull Harmless and Grabbett success was only a platinum credit card away.

Gerard could guess that his new friend had none of these attractive assets. Gerard did not yet have a business card and Frank's was a piece of paper, bearing a PO Box in Brighton but no street address.

"Brighton, eh?" Gerard said, trying desperately not to sound a little envious. "My girlfriend and I live in Blaxford."

Frank grinned happily. Here was an inferior being.

"I've just arrived from Adelaide," Gerard told him. "The cards are with the printer."

He had just dropped another two rungs on his social ladder, he could see it in Frank's eyes. Even those who desperately try to climb upwards, towards the bright lights of success, need somebody to look down on. It's only human.

"Oh, really?" he answered. "I always do them myself on the computer, it's simpler. Anyway, everyone knows who I am."

"What are you doing here?" Gerard asked.

Frank grinned mischievously, tapping the side of his nose with a knowing forefinger.

"Just checking up on the competition."

As they chatted about things of no consequence, Gerard gave him a quick and discreet inspection. The jacket was at least twenty years old, the shirt collar was rumpled and the St Kilda tie looked as if it had just come out of a close encounter with a Geelong supporter. He was the only man in the room wearing baggy jeans, and his shoes were badly worn. Somehow, Gerard did not think that Wistfull Harmless and Grabbett, or their young Blackberry wielding executives, were going to be very concerned by the possibility of having to compete with Frank Bliss.

"The coffee is lousy," Gerard commented. "In Adelaide, they would have served a crisp Sauvignon Blanc with the nibbles."

'They do have a bar here," Frank muttered. "But if you want alcohol you have to pay."

Gerard grabbed him by the arm and towed him towards the inviting wooden edifice and its array of bright lights and glittering bottles.

"My shout," Gerard announced.

Frank's eyes shone with delight.

Once served, they exchanged information about their business activities. Frank was surprised to learn that Gerard was mainly involved in export marketing and he seemed eager to show off his knowledge of South Australia's international trade. Gerard explained that the State exported wine, sheepskins, soft drinks, footballers, ug boots, crystallized fruit, table grapes, solar water heaters, barley, media magnates, fridge magnets and ambitious export consultants.

They had finished their first glass of Sauvignon Blanc and the barman was hovering, waiting for Frank to invite him to refill our glasses. He suddenly noticed the look of expectancy on both faces.

"Better not", he suggested, with an apologetic smile. "I have a business plan to work on this afternoon."

Gerard nodded glumly.

"You're probably right", he murmured.

He was just about to ask Frank about his business plan when the Master of Ceremonies invited everybody to sit down and to listen to words of wisdom. Messrs Wistfull Harmless and Grabbett themselves probably lived in Singapore, Paris or Seattle, but their local representatives were full of themselves and their employers' brilliant ideas. Graham Rockfast-Gluttony was still explaining how he had saved Maverton Haulage from extinction as Gerard crept out. He was surprised to hear Frank creeping behind him.

"Bloody boring," Gerard muttered.

Frank agreed, whispering that he could not understand how they could snare clients with that sort of rubbish. If Gerard compared poor Frank with the business advisers in thousand-dollar suits who had been telling them how wonderful they were over the last hour, he could well imagine that their services were in a different field to those offered by the mastermind from Brighton.

"How do we get to the car park?" he asked moving towards the lifts.

"2B I think", Frank replied. "I never bring my car into the city."

"Can I drop you off?" Gerard asked as they stepped together into the lift.

Frank nodded happily.

Frank liked the Honda Accord and ran his hands slowly over the leather dash, purring, as Gerard drove up the ramp. He decided not to explain that his Corolla was being serviced and that his girlfriend had lent him her wheels for the day. When they reached Brighton, Frank navigated the driver towards the front gates of a white two-storey mansion in what must have been one of the nicest streets in the suburb. Gerard whistled appreciatively, and Frank blushed.

"We must catch up," Gerard suggested as Frank stepped out of the car. "Can you give me your mobile phone number?"

"It's being repaired at the moment", Frank explained leaning through the car window. "But you have my home number on the card."

Gerard nodded, and Frank waved as he drove off. Gerard watched him in the rear vision mirror as he stood, still waving enthusiastically, as he turned the corner.

He ran into Frank quite by accident some four months later. He was shopping in Southland with his girlfriend when he saw him in the food hall eating an ice cream at a table with four kids. He introduced Sophie and saw thatFrank was suitable impressed.

"Your kids?" Gerard asked.

Frank frowned, then looked at the youngsters and laughed.

"Oh, no, I'm not interested in fatherhood."

At that moment an angry looking woman stormed over and told her children to come away from the table. She glared at Frank, as she reminded loudly them of her recommendations to keep away from strange men.

"I was just leaving anyway, and I'm not strange," Frank muttered lamely, tossing the unfinished ice cream into a rubbish bin. Then he turned to Gerard, perking up a happy smile.

"I'll walk to the car park with you."

They chatted idly until they reached the Honda.

"Where did you leave your car, Frank?" Gerard asked.

"My girlfriend's got it today", he explained as he opened the rear door of the Honda and slid on to the seat. "Mind dropping me off?"

Sophie looked a little annoyed but Gerard frowned, which was his way of begging her not to make a rude comment. She understood and sighed. Frank navigated again, but this time they dropped him off in front of an orange stucco home, in East Brighton. It looked like something out of a Zorro film. Sophie noticed that Gerard looked a little bemused as they drove off. He saw Frank in the rear vision mirror, waving them off.

"What's wrong?" she asked.

"The last time, I dropped him off at a different house," Gerard explained.

"Maybe he's moved in with a new girlfriend", she suggested with a cheeky grin.

Gerard shook my head and drove around the block to stop quietly at the top corner of the street they had just left. A few minutes later Frank walked quickly past on the opposite footpath, looking furtively left and right, although he passed their car without seeing them.

"Probably forgot to pick up a bottle of milk", Sophie suggested, but there was a wicked twinkle in her eye.

Two months later, Gerard decided to call Frank. He had picked up a contract with a company producing low-fat dairy products, and that they wanted him to research ideas for new lines, looking at what was happening overseas, Gerard suggested that Frank might be interested in doing some of the research over the Internet.

As he expected, Frank was delighted. Gerard quickly discovered that his partner did not have a computer for the moment and that his mobile phone was still 'on the blink', but Gerard magnanimously declared that he was happy to let him use his laptop and to work from his office at home. He told Frank that he would be out all day attending to clients. Frank's daily attire was simple: baggy jeans, a Jimmy Hendricks T-shirt and Nikes, probably because he came to work on a bicycle. However, he worked conscientiously and had soon established an interesting profile of the international market for dietary dairy products.

It became quickly obvious that Gerard's girlfriend overwhelmed poor Frank although Sophie herself was becoming severely frustrated with the unwelcome daily resident. Among other things, she was annoyed by the eagerness with which he drank their whisky and the number of times he seemed to end up having dinner with them.

She smiled when he explained about the houses in Brighton and Brighton East, and how they had caught him between two rentals.

"I never buy real estate," he explained. "I think it's an unproductive way of tying up your capital."

When his report was ready, Gerard told him that they had an appointment with the client, a certain Mr Attila Plattino. The day before the supposed appointment, Frank appeared at Gerard's front door, looking pale and agitated, and actually shaking like a leaf.

"Can I avoid the meeting?" he pleaded. "I'm not very good at this sort of thing."

Gerard told him that in that case he would only receive a minimum fee, a decision Frank accepted without protesting, jumping on to his old bicycle and pedalling away, with a look of relief on his face.

Sophie persuaded her companion to stop baiting Frank, and to forget his ailing computer, his broken mobile phone and his residential instability. He was a consultant, not a psychiatrist, she reminded him.

One Saturday morning, Sophie announced told him she had promised to lend some textbooks to a 'nice' girl she had met at the clinic and who was studying to be a paediatric nurse. They were going into Melbourne to catch up with some friends for lunch, so they stopped in Highett where the girl lived with her parents, on the way. It was a quiet street in an older part of the modest suburb. They lived in a neat little brick veneer with a pretty garden.

The only drawback seemed to be the derelict weatherboard cottage next door. There was a guy turning over a cabbage patch in the front yard with a fork, and Gerard would have recognized that Jimmy Hendricks T-shirt anywhere. At the front door was a very haggard looking blonde, wearing a partially unbuttoned but heavily stained pink blouse and grey baggy shorts. There was a cigarette butt hanging out of the corner of her mouth and a glass of white wine in her left hand. It was ten o'clock in the morning, but it was obviously not her first drop, to judge by the vile abuse she was screaming at the gardener.

Gerard was glad when Nancy invited them inside for a cup of tea, as he did not want to be a witness to Frank's humiliation. Their hostess apologised as she closed the front door.

"Sorry about the neighbours," she murmured. "They're really awful."

"They're new, are they?' Gerard asked.

She shook her head.

"No, they've been here for years. Molly used to work as a receptionist in a brothel in Dandenong until the boss chucked her out. Frank repairs lawnmowers."

There was nobody in the next-door garden when they left, but they could hear through an open window that Molly was still screaming abuse at poor Frank. Sophie pointed out a brown Lada in the driveway. It had no wheels.

"Strategic advisor, eh?" Sophie murmured sarcastically as they drove off. "Turf consultant, maybe?"

Gerard nodded glumly, without replying.

"Cutting edge!" she added, spitefully and laughed.

Attila Plattino was pleased with the job and gave Gerard his first Victorian cheque. To celebrate, he took Sophie to dinner *Chez Victor*. There was a new waiter, a man called Gaston from Paris and when Gerard spoke to him in his schoolboy French as he was setting us at the table, he was so delighted Sophie thought he was going to kiss her companion.

I wonder whether he ever worked at Faulty Towers." She asked. "Same height, same moustache . . ."

"Manuel was Spanish," Gerard reminded her.

He chose an Osso Bucco with couscous and spicy Mediterranean vegetables for both of them, accompanied by a Saint Joseph from *Cotes du Rhône* and Gaston declared that *Monsieur* was a *connaisseur!* People from neighbouring stared as Sophie sucked the marrow greedily.

Gerard ordered a second bottle of wine with the cheese platter, *Roquefort, Brie, Munster* and *Roblechon,* and later offered a generous tip to Gaston. As he helped them into the taxi (Sophie was singing

'Under the Bridges of Paris With You', very loudly), he wished them a pleasant night, with a heavy wink, and said that there would always be a table for 'Monsieur Gerard."

"Frank would have loved it," Sophie assured her friend when she reached the end of her song.

Gerard laughed.

Frank rang him about three weeks later, asking how things were going.

"I actually had a job for you last week," Gerard lied wickedly. "But I didn't have your mobile phone number."

Frank apologised.

"Would you believe that it's on the blink again?" he asked.

"Yes, Frank, Gerard told him sadly. "I can believe that."

About three months later Gerard was caught up in a traffic jam in Highett. The level crossing was closed, with a train stopped across the road. He parked the car and walked up towards the station, wondering how long he would have to wait. There was a frightened lady, explaining to a small group how she had been witness to a terrible accident.

"He just stepped off the platform in front of the incoming train," she sobbed, pale-faced. "It must have been a horrible way to die. A bloke standing at the end of the platform reckoned he was even smiling when he jumped."

Little pieces of paper had escaped from the dead man's pocket and were fluttering across the crossing. Gerard stooped and picked one up.

He would have recognised Frank's home-made business cards anywhere.

A TACTFUL FAREWELL

It was, as usual, a quiet afternoon in the Royal Victoria Club in Little Collins Street. Autumn leaves fluttered past the high windows and the sound of traffic passing outside was muted by the heavy stonewalls of the august building. No voice would be heard until dusk, when there would be calls for Glen Fiddich on the rocks, Dimple Haig and soda, London Gin with Indian Tonic Water or ales from the finest breweries in the world. Waiters would set out small silver platters bearing olives, potato crisps, or small *biscottes* covered in potted salmon, and might occasionally softly shake the shoulder of a distinguished member who had slipped away in the arms of Morpheus. Later, as the table lights began to gleam, Peter Deacon would appear and sit himself at the piano to play soft music from yesteryears. His repertoire had been the same for many decades, carefully chosen by the Club Committee after the Armistice that had ended the Second World War in Europe.

John Walsh, respected committee member, was sitting in his usual armchair in the member's lounge when Hector McTavish offered him the letter on the silver platter. Hand-delivered, it bore no postage mark but the envelope was of fine vellum and the handwriting denoted a person of genteel education. It had been written with an old-fashioned nib dipped in ink, and the letters were an assemblage of perfect circles, curves and flourishes. The sender's address was not on the back of the envelope.

"Intriguing," John murmured as he seized the silver paper knife offered to open the letter.

"Obviously from a lady of good standing," McTavish allowed himself to comment. "A distinguished but discerning person, if I may say so, sir."

McTavish could say so. He had been serving the members of the club, with a particular attention to the needs of John Walsh, for over thirty-eight years and was a man who knew much and said little. He was a trustworthy servant.

"Is the sun over the yardarm anywhere in the Empire?" John Walsh asked as he slipped the letter from the envelope.

"In Suva most certainly", McTavish affirmed with confidence. He knew that Mr Walsh's image of the Queen's Realm was still heavily dependent on the 1950 edition of the Boy's British Empire Annual.

"Then I'll have a brandy with soda and lemon", the gentleman decided.

McTavish allowed himself a mean smile, a simple task for a Highlander. John Walsh was an eccentric, allowing himself to drink spirits in the middle of the afternoon when others were enjoying a bergamot tea, but nobody in the club would dare to comment on his habits. He had been President of the club three times; he was a fine swordsman, and an outspoken critic of all things improper, indecent, inappropriate or posterior to Edward VII. Few club members had the courage to challenge his strongly voiced opinions. Thanks to John Walsh, women were still banned from the club, even those wearing pinstriped suits and monocles.

It was a pity that the members were not as careful with some of their new recruits, the manservant mused as he prepared the drink. People like that despicable Marcello Sabatini should not have been approved. Money does not buy good manners.

A few minutes later, McTavish reappeared silently, as if floating across the thick carpet, to place the glass on the pedestal table next to John's preferred armchair. The gentleman was deeply absorbed in the contents of the letter, and was wearing an angry frown. McTavish slipped away quietly. There were other club members sitting here and there in the large lounge, one or two with their faces covered by *The Age*. In one corner, a small group of four members was playing whist, while James Ernest Bummington and the Honourable Hugo Whistlewaite were sitting near the fireplace discussing, *sotto voce*, the latest changes on the Board of Globe Providence Insurance.

The Royal Victoria Club was a sanctuary of peace and tranquillity, an altar to good taste and fine manners. Voices were never raised in anger or excitement. Nobody wore thongs or Collingwood scarves. For more than a hundred years, the Club had steadfastly obeyed the rules of its founders who had decided that nobody born more than thirty miles from Spring Street would pass its doors.

At six o'clock, McTavish had been surprised to note that John Walsh had not called for his usual Bruichaddich Islay Single Malt of which he usually drank two doubles without ice before dinner. At seven o'clock, he decided to awaken him very gently to remind him of the tradition. The gentleman's eyes were firmly closed and his face was quite pale. As soon as McTavish touched his shoulder, he knew that something was seriously wrong.

He acted as the club expected a conscientious staff member to act. John Walsh was not the first gentleman to renounce his membership in such an irreversible manner, but nobody ever died in the members' lounge room. It was not done. He was removed discreetly a few minutes later, under a blanket and on a stretcher carried by two burly waiters, while the other members looking away tactfully. They had made incorrect assumptions and had decided that it was not fit to stare at a chap when he was leaving the Club in such an undignified manner, but if a chap cannot manage his drink then the staff must do what the staff must do.

When the waiters had picked up John Walsh, McTavish had seen the unusual letter fall from his hand, and he had snatched it up to hide it quickly in his trouser pocket. The Royal Victoria Club did not approve of gossip and despised scandal, and something in McTavish's bones told him that this letter would only cause difficulties if it fell into the wrong hands. Indeed, it may well have brought terrible news that could have contributed to the man's death.

An hour later, whispers floated from armchair to couch, slid across starched tablecloths or glided softly over the fine felt of the billiard tables confirming that John Walsh had left the Club, not because he was inebriated but more definitely, to join what some claimed to be a better world. All were Christians, although some members of the eminent fellowship privately believed that Heaven could not have better facilities than the library, the billiards room, the lounge and the dining room of the Royal Victoria Club. Some of the staff, like McTavish, had been there so long that they were almost part of the furnishings and if, one day one of them did not appear, in his or her usual place, the members would immediately note the discordance. Everything and everyone contributed to the delicate balance of harmony in this temple of good breeding: particularly staunch members like John Walsh.

McTavish slipped away at ten o'clock and walked quickly through the dark, wet streets towards the humble flat he shared with his cat, Angus, in Carlton. Once in his modest abode, he opened the bottle of Guinness he had hidden under his raincoat, lit the gas fire and settled himself in his favourite chair with Angus on his lap. Slowly, as if to better savour the moment, he slipped the mysterious letter from his pocket. As the flames hissed in the fireplace and the overweight cat purred on his knees, the Club's most faithful servant began to read the private letter addressed to the late John Walsh. It read as follows:

> *Dear Sir,*
>
> *I was distressed, but not surprised, to read the article in the Age reporting the speech you delivered to your friends in the John Green Memorial Society last Thursday. It was a gutless performance from a pompous charlatan, intent on telling the august gathering, a fellowship of portentous*

imbeciles, exactly what they wanted to hear. If the world were really to know the positive and negative effects prostitution has on your self-righteous society, perhaps a harlot such as I, Fifi Labelle, would be better suited to explain them. You talked of bestiality, of corruption and of depravity, when so often, the ladies of my world bring comfort and reassurance, and offer compassion and advice. If your arrogant and frigid concept of the world was not so merciless, men would find such joys and happiness within their own families without needing to confide their despairs and frustrations to strangers.

I should also point out that every whore, as you like to call us is, very often, somebody's wife and occasionally somebody's mother. They are also, invariably, somebody's daughter, and, for my shame, so am I. Although the grand-daughter of a man who prides himself of his rigid morality, I count many members of the Royal Victoria Club among my faithful visitors. I exercise my profession in a fine house, the Blue Orchid in South Yarra, and am proud of the happiness I provide.

My visitors all recognise me by the birthmark I have on my left buttock in the shape of a banana.

Fifi, Woman of Honour.

The letter ended here abruptly, and McTavish realised that when John Walsh had read that last sentence describing the birthmark he could well have died of shame and despair.

Three weeks later, Hector McTavish was sitting in the office of a reputed solicitor, Peter Hawke of Winston, Hawke and Crabtree. Beside him sat Mary Belinda, the charming grand-daughter of John Walsh, a young woman of twenty-eight years of age without sentimental attachments, it was said. They were there to learn of the dispositions of the will of the distinguished deceased gentleman. Miss Warble served three cups of Early Grey and placed a plate of Danish shortbread biscuits on the desk before leaving the room, closing the door quietly behind here. The solicitor coughed politely.

"There is a rather long preamble to my client's will which I have decided not to read. It contains comments about the morality of modern society and I have had two photocopies made for you. Here they are."

Hector and Mary Belinda accepted them without enthusiasm.

He then proceeded to read the will. John Walsh had bequeathed fifty thousand dollars to an orphanage in Sri Lanka and four thousand had been set aside for the care of his dog, Spinner, until his death. To his only descendant, his grand-daughter, Mary Belinda, he left his home in Rye, his fine collection of water paintings and his shares in a diamond mining company in Africa. He left fifty thousand dollars to the Club and Hector McTavish received a sum of one hundred and eighty thousand dollars as well as a vintage Sunbeam Talbot motor car.

After some minutes of polite conversation, the visitors left with the assurance that the solicitor would have all formalities completed before the end of the month.

"He was very generous with you, Hector," Belinda May commented on the footpath. "Will you be leaving the Royal Victoria?"

The faithful servant man smiled wistfully.

"I think I must. I have served it well, but I have little taste for the changes the younger members will inevitably introduce. There is talk of poker machines, dinner dances and bingo nights and these forms of entertainment are not part of my world. I will be looking for a little house in Ashmeadow to spend my final years."

Belinda May nodded and waved down a taxi, turning towards him to give him a friendly peck on the cheek before opening the door.

"Will I still see you Thursday afternoon, at the Blue Orchid, as usual?" she asked.

George squeezed her arm affectionately.

"Of course you will. I look forwards to our private meetings, as you well know."

And as she climbed into the taxi, he added.

"It was a pity that you had to mention that birthmark."

HOW A GOOD MAN LOST HIS WIFE

None of Tony Robinson's friends really understood why he had married Dulcinea. Some of them reckoned that when he lost his job as a driver with Maverton Haulage, the bottom had fallen out of his world and he needed a new challenge. A challenge was what he got.

Tony was probably still pondering about the wisdom of driving a truck full of frozen chicken into a river with a bottle of port in his right hand when he met his future wife in Melbourne in front of the Salvatore Dali exhibition. She had swept him off his feet in a few weeks. A bus load of Spaniards turned up for the wedding with heel-clicking dancers, palm-slapping singers and women with voluminous skirts, dark eyes and sultry smiles. Marital bliss waned, with the passion, within a few months.

According to Bob Murdoch at the Blaxford post office, a man of letters as he liked to call himself, Dulcinea was a Spanish name that meant sweetness. Her parents had made a bad choice. Dulcinea would have made a great bullfighter, a fantastic abattoir worker or a marvellous female wrestler, but a sweet, loving, caring wife she was certainly not. Everything about her was big: her hips, her arms, her four chins and her ego. After a few months of marriage Tony realised that there were two way of doing anything: the wrong way and Dulcinea's way. Invariably, Tony's way was always the wrong way.

Many married men in the same situation shrug their shoulders. They will tell you that about six months after the honeymoon this is how marital life slowly rots. In Tony's case it was sudden decay. Every decision he took, whether it was choosing fat free milk in the supermarket or buying a new screwdriver set at the hardware store, was not only wrong but his mistake was announced publicly, in a loud and unchallengeable voice. To add insult to injury, the reasons for his mistake were explained to anyone within a hundred metres, using expletives that placed grave doubts on his intelligence, his manhood and his sexual performance.

"You stupid fool," she would shout in front of a dozen clients at IGA."You know I NEVER drink that brand of milk."

And then, invariable, she would turn to the astonished spectators, clasping her crotch with an enormous hand.

"You know where his brain is? It's here, between his legs. And even there he doesn't use it too much!"

All this was delivered with a strong Spanish accent which encouraged Barry Pescia, who was Tony's best mate at the joinery, to suggest in a whispered voice that Dulcinea was a fine example of why immigration into Australia should have been limited to people from the British Isles. Dulcinea should have stayed in Spain to fight Mussolini, he reckoned. Barry was reputed for his excellent horse racing tips, but his mastery of the history of European dictators was less convincing.

Tony got a job with selling life insurance for Globe Providence because somebody had to make a living. Dulcinea stayed at home and moaned.

A year later, Tony and Dulcinea disappeared for a week's holiday. It appeared that his wife had developed an irresistible urge an urge to visit the 'Top End', to see the desert, the gorges, the Aboriginals and the crocodiles, so *El Pendejo*[6] loaded La *Ponderosa*[7] into the *Pajero* and they set off into the midday sun. On the 30th September, Tony reappeared, alone, wearing a big, big smile.

We had to wait for Happy Hour in the Blaxford Arms the following Friday night to tackle him. Bob Murdoch had been spreading the rumour that she had asked Tony to stop the car about three hundred clicks from Alice Springs to have a pee and that he had taken off in a cloud of dust while she had her size 28 knickers round her ankles. Not many people thought that Tony would do that sort of thing. Jack, Tony's boss was adamant.

"Tony wouldn't hurt a fly," he insisted. "Even a Spanish fly. He just cops shit all day with a smile on his face."

Brian, who was Tony's cousin, was not so sure.

"A man is a man," he stated with all the wisdom he could muster.

We nodded, knowing that this important philosophical statement was a precursor of bigger things.

"He sits there, listening to all those insults, and then, suddenly, something inside of him snaps," Brian explained. "In a burst of madness, he strikes!"

Brian's gesture nearly knocked his beer off the bar and Maureen, the barmaid, squealed in fright. A few of us nodded. But you should have seen the look on our faces when Tony walked into the pub.

"She's been eaten by crocodiles," he announced quietly, without emotion, in reply to Brian's question.

At that point, eight of us got together and set up a fund of fifty dollars that we gave to Maureen and we told her to keep filling Tony's glass every time it was empty. We wanted to know everything! The game of darts came to an abrupt end, the TV was switched off, and the crowd stood around the bar, ready for the story. It began simply.

"You see, we had pulled into a little town on a river estuary west of Darwin," Tony explained. "I was sitting on the sand at the foot of

---

6 A weak, stupid man, often cuckolded by his wife.

7 The powerful woman

the embankment and Dulcinea had slipped on her bikini to stretch out on the ground closer to the water's edge."

I closed my eyes, trying to imagine that voluminous and almost naked Spanish anatomy lying in the mud.

"She moaned, of course,"Tony explained.

Several of us nodded. It was something she did very well. He remembered that she had moaned loudly about the heat as she lay, sprawled on her back, in the wet sand. He had not replied. He had warned her that the weather would be hot and humid, but missus-know-all would not listen.

"For me, a holiday is my deck chair, a six-pack and the latest edition of *Classic Detective Stories",* Tony explained. "And if Dulcinea wanted to spend her day on her back, toasting her cellulite on a muddy beach, gazing through her Ray-Bans at a dark blue sky, moaning incessantly, that was fine by me."

We looked at one another, more than surprised. That must have been the longest and bravest speech Tony had made since his marriage.

"I had just reached the bit where *Pierre Lafleur*, Nouméa's most popular detective, had opened the wardrobe door to find six terrified nuns and a delighted second-hand car salesman hiding from an imaginary chainsaw killer when Dulcinea let out an almighty shriek. Slowly and carefully, I marked my page and put down the book."

We nodded. He had always been careful and methodical, our Tony. "For God's sake, what's happening? she had screamed. I told her to stay calm. There are three large crocodiles that must have come up out of the water without me noticing, and one of them is holding her foot in his mouth."

There was now total silence in the public bar. Brian was banging his empty glass on the bar counter calling for a refill but Maureen was too busy listening to this terrifying story. We were all impatiently waiting for the next episode.

"Lovely animals, crocodiles,' Jack commented. "Make great handbags."

Everybody shushed him.

"She begged me to chase off the crocodile,"Tony explained."She was turning and twisting in pain, but what could I do?"

We nodded sympathetically, but I noticed that there was not a tear in his eyes. With a sigh, he reminded us that he measured 173 centimetres and weighed sixty-eight kilos so there was no way he was going to wrestle, single-handed, an eight-metre crocodile. We murmured that we understood, although eight metres sounded like a bit of an exaggeration.

"I told her that if she stayed calm and didn't draw attention, he would probably go away and join his friends," Tony said. "I tried to use a soothing tone to settle her."

Bob Murdock seemed to have strangled himself with his last gulp of beer and rushed out to the toilet, coughing desperately. I'm always careful not to laugh when I'm drinking.

As Maureen poured him another beer, Tony explained that his wife had screamed loudly that the beast was going to drag her down in to the water but she was wrong: at that very moment, the animal moved off, taking only the foot with him.

"I stood up,"Tony explained."I called out and told her that it was probably less painful now. He said that her reply was in Spanish and that he could not offer a correct translation, although the accompanying gestures were very explicit."

Barry patted him on the shoulder.

"We know, we know," he told his friend gently. "We know how she used to treat you, but she was still your wife. Let it all out, it will make you feel better."

Tony nodded gratefully.

"The big animal was looking at me and chewing thoughtfully," he explained. "You could hear the bones cracking. Behind me, on the embankment, people were beginning to scream and gesticulate. I stood up and made a cone with my hands in front of my mouth. 'I'm sure it's not as bad as it looks,' I shouted in their direction. 'If somebody has a mobile phone, could they call the ranger or whoever looks after crocodiles?'"

'Good thinking, Tony", Barry Pescia murmured, and Jack nodded.

Tony pursued his strange story.

"I saw a guy wave that he had understood and I suggested that it would be best not let the kids come down as they tend to be easily frightened. I then turned back to my wife. The poor darling was looking quite pale and I could hear her moaning very loudly. I called out, asking her to make less noise because she might draw the attention of the other two reptiles."

He said that he told her that for the moment she had only lost a foot, it was not the end of the world.

"I was trying to be supportive," he muttered.

We looked at one another, nodding our approval. Tony had been remarkably brave and calm. Courageously, he continued his story

"She asked me to come down towards her and to drag her out of harm's way. I explained that I would never have made it on my own because she was too heavy. I offered to toss her a couple of soluble Panadol. She told me where I could shove the Panadol, but I was not offended. I knew it was the pain taking over. She shouted so loudly that she interrupted the crocodile's meal, and he stopped munching and raised his head. I was terrified."

Barry and I agreed that when Dulcinea was in a bad mood and began to shout at her husband, it could be quite frightening.

"I meant afraid of the crocodile, not of her!" he snapped at us, angrily.

A large crowd had gathered around us now and the pub was packed. Some people were whispering to one another while others were hissing at them to shut up. Tony took a long draft of beer from his glass and wiped his lips with the back of his hand.

"They are quite intelligent animals and this one looked really, really angry", he explained. "She should have shut up, it could have been better if she had shut up!"

"She never could shut up, we all know that," Brian commented softly. "It wasn't your fault, mate."

There was a loud murmur of ascent in the pub. Feeling the unspoken support around him seemed to give Tony more courage. He had surely known that many had laughed behind his back at the rough treatment his Spanish wife had dealt out; perhaps he was ready to show that the victim could be compassionate towards the bully. It made a good story. His voice was louder, more assertive, as he pursued his narrative.

"Dulcinea went on abusing me," he said, sadness in his voice. "She reminded me that we had planned to go dancing that evening in a club in Darwin. I tried to reassure her, suggesting that she could always hop around on one foot. I did not tell her that as we spoke the crocodile had slid slowly closer and was now staring at the other foot, the one still attached to her body."

When he paused, the silence in the sub was stifling.

"Suddenly the animal lunged!" He shouted

Maureen screamed, but Tony pressed on, undaunted. He could feel the tension around him. He obviously knew that those listening needed to know the rest, quickly, urgently.

"I heard her scream," he sobbed. "I heard the crunching of bones. I must have been going mad, because I distinctly remembered thinking, stupidly, that somebody with a camera could have taken some shots that would have been snapped up by a toothbrush manufacturer."

Barry patted his shoulder to comfort him, but other people in the bar were exchanging worried looks. It sounded as if Tony was going completely off his rocker, but nobody dared interrupt him.

Tony's wiped away his tears and continued with determination.

"Dulcinea's screams were frightening the people on the embankment and they had begun to pack things in their cars, shouting fearfully at one another. A fat lady called out, asking if she was in much pain. I tried to reassure her, saying her that once the foot was detached it would not be too bad. I insisted again that they should take the children away, if not they would be paying for psychologists for the rest of their lives. 'And he might find them more appetizing. I imagine that a little four or five year old would be quite tender.' the fat lady told me before asking if she should call Today Tonight. I told her that I was not sure. It depended what they're prepared to offer, I said, but if you do, warn them that my wife hasn't had a manicure this month and her hair's a bit of a mess."

Some of the people in the bar were beginning to murmur. It seemed almost as if the drama had driven Tony crazy, judging by the hard-headed decisions he claimed to have made at such a terrible moment.

Tony raised his voice to silence them.

"My poor wife was now looking very pale. The beast had moved back down towards the water with the second foot."

He giggled.

"It reminded me of Sally, my old Labrador, who would spend hours in the garden playing with an ox bone."

Some of the crowd began to leave the bar, shaking their heads sadly. Tony looked disappointed.

"Don't you want me to finish the story?" he called out.

A couple of old mates nodded and he took a deep breath before resuming.

"I tried to cheer her up," he said. "I told her that I was proud of her courage and that the crocodile had taken off the second foot almost at exactly the same height as the first. I added that she would be able to get a matching pair of prostheses that would be quite smart."

"That would have cheered her up," Brian thought aloud.

Tony nodded happily.

"It did. She even found the force to smile and to ask if they would come in natural colours. I told her that we would probably find something to match her lovely tan."

His mates looked at one another and shook their heads. They could never have imagined that Tony was so cold-blooded. It just showed what years of hen-pecking can do to a man. He continued, relentless.

"By that time, most of the cars had left, but there were still two spectators, a man with a digital camera, and the fat lady with her mobile phone. The man said he would send his film to Sky News and ask them to send him a copy. I waved, to show that I had understood, marvelling at how complete strangers could be so helpful in times of adversity. Then the woman called out that the third crocodile was on the move, hoping to join the feed and that it was a pity that her husband did not have a rope to pull her to safety with the Land Cruiser."

"Good thinking, "Bob Murdock said enthusiastically.

Tony shook his head.

"it was a stupid idea. Trying to tie a rope around Dulcinea while the crocodile were feeding could be a very dangerous activity. In any case, it was too late. At that moment, Dulcinea screamed and fainted. The second crocodile had grabbed her left leg just below the knee. He chewed for a while and then snapped it off.'

There was a loud bang as Maureen, the barmaid fainted and her head connected with the wooden floorboards. Tony waited patiently while Bob Murdock carried her out the back.

My poor darling was now losing a lot more blood," he told us. "But I was still hopeful that if the rangers came soon they could still get her to safety and patch up what was left. The man had put down his camera and was vomiting in the grass. At that moment, three rangers turned up in a Mitsubishi twin cab four-wheel drive."

"Love that car," somebody said in the pub, but nobody laughed.

Tony ignored the comment and continued.

"I saw one ranger slipping and sliding to down the embankment, rifle in hand. The third crocodile had now grabbed Dulcinea by the remaining leg and was dragging her towards the water. She was no longer screaming and I decided that she had overcome the pain barrier. I was so proud of her. It was an important moment. The other two rangers stood on either side of me as my darling wife slid slowly towards the water. One of them told me that his colleague would have to shoot, as the man near the river raised his rifle."

Nobody spoke in the bar. Maureen must have been feeling better because we could hear her vomiting in a bucket in the back room. Tony sighed.

"The man below fired, and I saw my darling's body jump with the impact of the bullet. 'There, there, now she won't suffer,' the ranger next to me whispered, patting me gently on the shoulder. 'We can't kill the crocodile; it's a protected species.'"

We looked at one another in shocked silence while Tony sobbed.

"Afterwards, we sat on the embankment and let the three splendid animals finish their feast," he explained. "I have to admit that we were all crying as we watched my little honey-bunch disappear, little by little, in the blood-red sunset.

Barry Pescia squeezed his friend's arm It was a sad moment He had told us the whole story with such compassion that we were all moved not only by the disappearance of his wife, but also by his talent as a story-teller.

He ploughed on, wiping the tears from his red eyes with a sodden handkerchief.

"When the animals, stomachs full, slipped back into the water, the rangers put what was left of Dulcinea in a big black bag that they then tossed into the back of the truck", he told us. "Then we all went down to the local where we drank together several solemn toasts to my departed wife. But worse was to come."

We waited with bated breath. The glasses were empty, but nobody wanted a drink.

"We went back to the truck when the pub closed," Tony whispered sadly. "The plastic bag with what was left of my tender and loving wife had disappeared. One of the rangers reckoned that a dingo had taken her away. The Funeral Plan I had taken out was a total waste of money."

There was nothing more to tell. Barry Pescia, Brian and Jack took Tony home.

The rumour started when Barry Pescia told a few close friends that he had seen Tony twice in Melbourne during that week he was supposed to have been with his wife in the Territory. He had been clowning around with a couple of tarty looking girls in St. Kilda, and he had not seen Barry.

Then tongues started wagging faster. Bob Murdock wrote to a friend in Darwin about the tragic accident and his mate wrote back saying that there had been no death by crocodile reported in the local press. A few days later, Brian's dog, Tracker, broke into Tony's back yard and started wailing as he dug up the compost heap. Blaxford police were called in and found among the vegetable peelings and other scraps, large pieces of Dulcinea. A large parsnip had been jammed into her mouth.

When they took Tony away, he had a big grin on his face. We had not seen him so happy for a long time. Barry thought that he was probably proud to be Blaxford's first murderer.

A MAGNIFICENT FAREWELL

As Christine O'Reilly walked solemnly towards the microphone, the people in the church fell silent. The men held themselves straight, gazing ahead, their eyes shiny with sadness. The women sobbed loudly into delicate lace handkerchiefs, their tears hidden behind black veils. The senior officers from the Vice Squad, in dress uniform, were solemn and respectful, the Commissioner and the Police Minister stood with their heads bowed.

In one corner stood a group of young women, dressed in black, but still quite provocatively for such a solemn event. They were Marcello's girls, the best that money could buy, and proud of their reputation. In another corner stood a small group of young girls, all dressed in virginal white. They were members of the choir of the School of Saint Therese. Marcello had been a generous benefactor of the school, which is why they were there to sing songs of praise and faith. The presence of a bishop and two priests confirmed, if necessary, the powers once wielded by the man who now lay in the splendid white coffin. A mountain of flowers and wreaths covered the casket, bearing messages of love and friendship, in Italian and in English. Many promised revenge for the dreadful crime committed on his person.

Christine cleared her throat and spoke.

"Many of you will not know me. My name is Christine, and I was not born in Naples, or Rome or Palermo, but in County Cork. I was Marcello Sabatini's woman. I speak today on behalf of his mother, an old lady who merits the respect of our community. She is tired of reading those bad things people write about her son in the press, and she is angry that even SBS talks about this fine member of the Italian community of Melbourne as if he was the worst gangster the city has ever seen. Camellia Sabatini believes that the son she has just lost was not a bad boy; but a saint and an example of righteousness and generosity for us all."

The bishop coughed, very softly, but Christine ignored the interruption. The donation to the Church, a wad of green notes in a white envelope, had bought her the right to talk. The roof was in dire need of repair.

"Camellia is a fine woman and a proud mother, and she wants people to recognise Marcello for the good son he was. She wants them to know that Marcello always looked after his family and that if sometimes people got killed it was only because he had many loyal friends who wanted to protect his reputation. You will remember when Paolo Pannacotta, Giovanni Pancetta and Arturo Mozarella joined their Creator, all together, just four years ago, after an incident in a restaurant in Fitzroy. At their funeral, the biggest wreath was from my Marcello, and everyone agreed that his '*Buon Viaggio*[8]' message to his three friends was touching and full of love. Because Marcello owned the shotgun that killed them, as well as the supposed executioner's getaway car, the press harassed him for more than two years. Only the vice squad had faith, knowing from the start that it was a case of collective suicide and that Marcello was at home with his mother that evening."

The senior officer from the vice squad blushed and shuffled his feet. The bishop shuddered. Paolo Palladino's widow burst into tears

---

8 Bon Voyage

and dropped her head on Carlo Cambisi's shoulder. Christine pointed a trembling finger in their direction.

"See how Marcello's cousin, the handsome and God-fearing Carlo, comforts the widow of a man he respected," she called out. "After the death of Paolo, he employed her as receptionist in the Pink Heaven, 14 Hovercraft Street, in Collingwood; open every day from 10 am. to midnight, no bookings necessary. Is that the act of a pitiless accomplice to a mass murder?"

One of Marcello's girls, a tall blonde with a voluptuous figure, stood up and curtsied, but the small Asian girl next to her tugged her arm and forced her to sit down. The girls from the Pink Heaven had been taught to be discreet. The bishop frowned a warning, obviously not approving the promotion of a house of sin in a building devoted to the praise of God. Two of the girls from the Saint Therese choir giggled, but Christine pursued her oration, ignoring the distractions.

"Family problems started in Naples, after the War, when Marcello's father, Bernardo, did business with a bad man, Paolo Carcopino. They were dealing in American cigarettes, French silk stockings and Albanian hostesses. They had a big disagreement about a shipment of Lucky Strike to Libya and Bernardo's gun went off. Marcello's father was still sobbing and holding his good friend in his arms when his employees dragged him away to safety. Good friends hid the family for a few months in the hills in Sicily, then Bernardo got some nice papers and they were shipped out to Australia on a lovely white Lloyd Triestino ship."

Several people in the congregation sighed, nodded to one another and a little old lady murmured 'Lloyd Triestino' wistfully.

"It was the Oceania!" Marcello's mother called out proudly.

The Bishop frowned and Christine resumed her story.

"They were very proud of their new passports, and landed in Australia as Mr and Mrs Bernardo Sabatini. Marcello's mother was very angry when the press called her teenage son by the terrible nickname they have given him, 'Marcello Bordello and his Murderous Cello'. He was always proud to carry his father's name, even if it was not the real one. His mother told me that he has never carried a machine gun in that cello case; he had too much respect for great music. Later, he even encouraged his son to learn to play the banjo."

She stopped for a moment to wipe away a tear and then resumed her story.

"People talk a lot about the great invasion of Italian migrants after the war. They do not stop to think about how lucky they were that they came. The 'wogs' built roads and dams and railways and houses and public buildings all over the country. They made prosciutto, salami, and pasta and showed us all why a meal at a table with friends and family is not a sad, silent English event but a noisy, laughing party."

This statement provoked a round of timid applause, and the bishop glared at the community. The church was also the place of worship of English Catholics and he did not want to provoke ethnic warfare. Christine smiled and pursued her mission.

"When young Marcello was a teenager he was already popular with the girls. He was handsome, like his father, and he charmed them with his accent, his beautiful smile, and his flattering compliments. While the Ozzie boys courted girls like bulldozer drivers attacking a virgin forest, Marcello charmed them with words, caresses and flowers. When a pimple-ridden teenage Smith, O'Brien's or Mackenzie proposed a 'quickie' in the back of the ute with a rude laugh, Marcello talked about passion and love on a moonlit beach with a voice like silk."

The 'quickie in the back of a ute' made one of the young priests giggle, and the bishop turned round to wag an admonishing finger in his direction. He reminded himself that this young man had been one of the more turbulent seminary trainees, caught twice 'on the tiles' when he should have been in his chaste bunk, playing only with his rosary.

"Marcello Sabatini's gentle attitude towards women was probably the reason why the State government allowed him to own several legal brothels under different names", Christine explained. "All the girls loved him, and he granted special discounts to important people and politicians. After all, as Marcello said, ministers, important businessmen and senior public servants devote much of their lives to serving the community and are entitled to a little relaxation and loving care in return."

A few of the distinguished personalities in the front row began to shuffle their feet and examine their shoelaces. Some of them had even crossed paths, inadvertently, in one of the concealed parking areas behind one or another of Marcello's houses of relaxation. Luckily, they were all Rotarians, and respected one another's indiscretions. On the other hand, there seemed to be a hissed and angry conversation going on in a row further back, between the Mayor of Blaxford and his wife. The bishop glared and the mayor's wife stopped hissing but she continued to glare at her husband with anger.

"There was competition, of course, often by illegal operators", Christine declared. "But Marcello, aware of his civic duties, always warned the local councils. Because they often lacked the resources necessary to enforce the law, Marcello set up a security company to help them and he never billed a council for the service. He even offered jobs to some of the poor girls caught up in those terrible illegal cat-houses. Marcello had friends in high places and saw that nobody challenged their rights to earn an honest living in a country that greeted them with open arms."

At that moment, the Mayor for Blaxford apparently decided to leave the ceremony, in some haste. He ran, crouched over, holding his hands over his head to protect himself from the blows distributed by an angry wife with a heavy handbag. Christine paused for a moment, waiting for the laughter to die down, before pursuing.

"Marcello gave generously to the Police Associations and helped the widows and orphans who had lost a husband or a father in the course of their duty. He ate and drank with famous men, dined with Premiers, Ministers and Police Commissioners, and donated generously to political parties, hospitals, football clubs, jockeys and charities. He was chairman of the Globe Providence Insurance, he created the Kitchen Man franchise, and he owned Maverton Haulage. Marcello arrived here as the son of a poor migrant and eventually created hundreds of jobs in this country."

The mourners nodded, and several 'hear, hears' emanated from the congregation. Then Christine's tone changed. She became assertive and she hit the palm of her hand with her fist to punctuate her statements.

"Marcello Sabatini was a great man. He nearly became a Companion of the Order of Australia and was close to being elected to the board of the Carlton Football Club. If he did not attend Kevin's 20/20 summit in Canberra, it was because he had a cold that weekend."

Christine's eyes sparkled with anger as she shouted her closing phrase.

"How can we believe that such a fine man, the proud son of courageous and God-fearing Italian migrants, a shining light in our community, would have shot himself in a Blaxford V-line train? He hated trains, and when he visited his girls in Blaxford, it was always in his armour-plated Beamer! Also, must I remind you, a fervent Catholic does not take his own life? Life is a gift from God."

The bishop clapped and the congregation rose to its feet as the Police Minister and the head of the Vice Squad led the hymn of praise. Marcello's mother stood up, hands clenched across her chest, eyes raised to the dome. She knew that her Creator would hear her prayer and would help Chief Inspector Carola Tamburo nail the *figlio di puttana*[9] who had killed her son in a speeding train.

As the coffin slowly passed between the mourners on the shoulders of eight men in black suits wearing wrap-around sunglasses, the choir broke out with the deceased man's favourite song:

"Que sera, sera, whatever will be will be, the future's not ours to see, que sera sera."

The chant stopped suddenly and a shocked silence fell upon the assembly. From inside the coffin, Marcello's mobile, a Kawashima Cosmic Deluxe, still in the pocket of his best suit, began to ring. His mother fell to her knees, calling out her thanks. As the coffin hit the

---

9 Son of a whore

floor and the bearers grabbed for their holsters, the ringing stopped. A short conversation was heard from within the coffin, and everyone in the congregation recognised that one of the voices was that of Marcello himself.

"*Marcello*?" asked a deep voice.

"Si, Signore," the dead man replied.

"Hurry yourself! The gates close in one hour."

There was a sigh.

"*Mia mogle é chiaccerone,*[10]" the dead man explained.

There was laughter from the deep voice.

"*E allora*? All women are chatterboxes. I designed them that way! *Avanti!* Remember, you have one hour left!"

There was a familiar click as the communication ceased. The bishop was on his knees, eyes raised towards the roof, lips feverishly offering silent prayers.

"Did you hear, did you hear?" Father Griscelli whispered to Father Fratelli. "Our Lord speaks Italian, even with a Sicilian accent!"

The armed pall-bearers were not concerned with linguistics. They knew that they had less than an hour to get Marcello to his last place of rest and they lost no time. The inhabitants of Fitzroy saw the strangest of funeral processions that day. The hearse was roaring down the street, headlights flashing, and horn blaring. Some mourners were sprinting behind, the ladies with their high-heeled shoes in their left hands while their right hands clasped hats prepared by Melbourne's best milliners. The two priests followed them on a scooter. The drug squad followed in their unmarked cars, tyres smoking.

"Another drug bust down at the cemetery", one shopkeeper was heard to whisper to a customer.

At the burial plot, there was a hurried prayer, a hasty waving of the aspergillum, and the diggers were shovelling the earth back into the hole before the coffin had even hit the bottom.

---

10 My wife is a gasbag

As dusk fell on the cemetery, the familiar sound of rifles being loaded could be heard over the chatter of the grasshoppers. Two guards remained, with firm instruction from Bernardo Sabatini; Marcello's nephew who was worried what might happen if his uncle arrived at the Pearly Gates after closing time. He imagined his uncle appearing the next morning in the boardroom of Global Providence Insurance to reclaim his chair. All Bernardo's careful planning would have been futile.

"If the old bastard tries to climb out, shoot to kill!" were his vehement instructions.

The two guards nodded silently.

THE MAGIC POTION

Bernard McNamara was neither a happy man nor the most popular man in Sutton Vale. His wife hated him, his colleagues laughed at him and his boss was always hinting that he could find better pastures elsewhere, in Mongolia, for example. Poor Bernard was not the most popular accountant at Maverton Haulage. Every morning, when he gazed at that questionably handsome but obviously unlucky man staring back at him from the shaving mirror, he knew that things were going to get worse. Well, worse than yesterday, and probably better than tomorrow.

To fight ill fate, he had stuck a popular saying above his shaving mirror: it told him that today he was reborn; it was the first day of his new life. His wife had written underneath, in crimson lipstick 'then go back to your mother and enjoy it!' He had been tempted, but he realised that he could hardly tell his mother that she had been right all along and that his marriage had been the disaster she had forecast.

Clementine, his wife, was not a happy woman, either. She told everyone, even those who did not want to know, that her husband was a failure: at work, at home, in the kitchen and in the tool shed. Moreover, when she mentioned the phrase 'tool shed', she accompanied it with a very unladylike gesture that explained exactly what she was implying. Many of the men of her generation, who had known her in her youthful, lustful years, could confirm that Clementine was not the kind of lady who liked lengthy diplomatic discourse and amorous promises. Clementine Lamoutarde, now Clementine McNamara, had always been a woman of action. When Clementine went to Captain Snore in Blaxford to choose a new bed and bounced up and down on the mattress, the salesman knew what was on her mind.

For Bernard, this morning was just another Monday morning. The coffee was tepid, the eggs congealed, the toast burnt and the news was bad: Australia had been demolished by Sri Lanka in the World Cup, Kylie Minogue had twisted her ankle during a concert in Liverpool and the Reserve Bank had put up interest rates. And if that wasn't enough to ruin a bloke's day, he read that the Hawks' new star player had had his face banged a few times against the bonnet of his new Lexus by a jealous husband.

"The bastard will probably get a suspended sentence," Bernard muttered through the Age to a wife who was deeply engrossed in a story concerning the latest scandalous love affair of a female federal senator. She didn't reply, and he lowered the paper very slowly to make sure she was there. She stood out starkly against the virginal white setting of their modern kitchen/family room.

She was, munching seaweed biscuits and reading trash, hiding her irresistible beauty behind a thick layer of miraculous rejuvenating cream made in Paris and based on zebra testicles and grated papaya. She had covered her head with purple curlers, and the overall look was that of an OVNI that had just landed in a plate of cottage cheese.

He sighed.

Twenty-eight years of marriage had provided nothing but frustrations. Two kids at University with unsustainable financial needs, a holiday home in Whittlewood they never used, a Volvo V60 with a cracked windscreen, a depleted libido and a sex-hungry wife having an affair with a plumber.

He sometimes wondered how he, once an ambitious and charming man, could have screwed up his life. Marriage had been a disaster (yes, mother!), but he had been too young and too innocent to envisage sex without marriage. Once married to the female volcano, he had quickly discovered that her sexual hunger was insatiable. Philosophically, Bernard described himself as a matrimonial pacifist. More spitefully, his mates at work called him a wimp.

Clementine, the snob, loved a little vulgarity in her life. She had a passionate hunger for tradesmen in stained overalls, touting a voluminous tool kit, offering a twenty-four hour service.

"Have you seen my new quilt cover?" she would ask the new apprentice electrician sent round by Brian Hughes and Associates, dragging him by the arm towards the master bedroom.

"Have you seen my new shower fixture?" she would ask the plumber from Captain Tap as she suddenly appeared, damp and desirable, from behind the shower screen.

"I do wish the tradesmen would stop leaving their stuff everywhere," Bernard would complain feebly in the evening when stepping on a screwdriver into the walk-in wardrobe.

"Stop moaning and come to bed," Clementine would reply in that voice he knew so well and which refused any excuses.

Bernard was sacrificed occasionally on the altar of lust with little personal enthusiasm. To even remotely satisfy her demands, he would have had to race home every day to tear off her clothes, to throw her on to the king-size bed with surrounding mirrors and to ravage her frantically for a couple of hours.

Bernard was not that kind of guy.

After work, he usually had a few quiet beers with his mates in the pub. Then he would go home, stick his feet under the table and ask what was for tea. He was not adverse to a little nooky on a Saturday night, but everything he did he undertook gently, carefully, without breaking into a sweat. Bernard intended to lead a long, tranquil and healthy life.

Clementine was a determined woman. She firmly believed that a husband should be encouraged to perform his contractual obligations with enthusiasm, while painters, plumbers, gas fitters and turf maintenance experts provided enjoyable and sometimes exciting complements.

One Tuesday morning, Bernard received a curious mail in his office. It arrived in the hands of a cocky young secretary with a mini skirt hardly covering her bottom who put it on his desk, opened of course, and with a very suggestive giggle. Ten minutes later, he could hear the roars of laughter in the outer office and he was told by a close friend, that afternoon, that the Manager of Corporate Communications had been obliged to temporarily suspend a seminar on funeral insurance to allow the attendees to withdraw to the footpath to cackle hysterically. Cocky secretaries with short skirts loved to gossip, and she had opened the envelope, inadvertently, before handing in to Bernard.

It had contained several pieces of paper. The first was an A3 leaflet declaring that New Life Adhesive Wonders were ten times more powerful than any other impotency medication guaranteeing 'rock hard results whenever needed'! Shocked, but interested, he shoved the rest of the information into his pocket and fought his way past an office full of people obviously sharing a good joke to lock himself into a toilet cubicle where he would be able to read in peace.

He discovered that the miracle product consisted of two adhesive strips containing secret medicines inherited from the Incas. All the patient had to do was to stick them to his temples. This magic potion delivered stimulating incentives that reached the brain within five minutes, and the patient would achieve almost immediately 'lift-off' for an unwavering period of twenty-four hours.

He read on.

The promoters of this 'miraculous product claimed that it eliminated fatigue and indifference or the need to invent a migraine. Quoted references boasted new-found youth. Richard's wife in Albury found it so good that she ordered a box for her boss. After using Adhesive Wonders, Len from Cremorne is now invited every Saturday evening to key-ring swapping parties right across the North

Shore. Rob in the Adelaide Hills claimed that his girlfriend, like Oliver Twist, keeps asking for more.

Bernard stuck the reply-paid envelope and the application for a free thirty-day trial into his trouser pocket. Back in the office, he tossed the rest of the 'offending' material on to his secretary's desk and told her to throw it away, unless she knew anybody on the staff who might be incapacitated. Her wicked grin told him that she did and was staring at him right now. Clementine's activities at the last office Christmas Party had not been forgotten.

That evening, he posted his order, giving the local pub as his postal address, because the owner was a good friend. Firstly, he did not want his wife, the plumber, other service providers and his colleagues to know that he was going to test the product. Secondly, he had read that the product could also work on some women, and he knew that if Clementine opened the parcel before he got home, it could mean sudden death for most of the tradesmen on her call list.

Bernard loved his wife, and hoped that the miracle remedy would allow him to satisfy her needs and eliminate the need for external service providers. For Bernard, love was something more than just sex.

An anonymous small parcel wrapped in brown paper and addressed to him arrived in the pub on Thursday. The hotelier winked as he handed it to him. Bernard spent a restless night, tossing and turning, wondering about the new, virile life that would begin at dawn. Heart galloping at high speed, he stuck two of those wonderfully rejuvenating strips to his temples the following morning, while he was shaving. Five minutes later, he had to step back to avoid having an inappropriate relationship with the washbasin. He took another three steps backwards and could not believe what he saw in the mirror.

He raced down the stairs, shaving cream still covering part of his face to confront his wife with the stark evidence.

"Clementine!" he shouted as he burst into the kitchen.

He had forgotten that the plumber was supposed to call in early that morning, once again to fix a leaking tap, and he and Clementine turned to stare at him.

"Don't worry, George," Clementine told the plumber, patting his arm affectionately. "It only happens once a year."

Then turning back to her husband, she added spitefully.

"I'm busy Bernard. Go away!"

The contempt he detected in her voice and the way she let her hand stay on the plumber's arm, would, normally, have deflated the ambitions of any ordinary husband. But not today. Not this Bernard with the adhesive wonders stuck to his temples.

"Come upstairs immediately," he shouted. "Call the office to say I won't be in this morning."

He spun around, forgetting his new anatomical dimensions, and banged himself painfully against the kitchen door. Upstairs, he stretched out on his back on the bed, ambitions pointing firmly towards the ceiling, and waited. Half an hour later, he heard the plumber's van pull out of the drive. Another half hour passed and he heard the garage door lift and Clementine's Renault Clio back down the driveway.

Furious, he leapt from the bed and raced downstairs, seriously hurting himself once again at the bend in the staircase. He burst out into the front garden, desperate trying to catch his wife, but it was too late. The neighbour's daughter, who was just hopping into her Getz, saw him and screamed, pulling the car door closed and pushing down the safety button.

He went back into the house and within ten minutes discovered two things: first of all, there was no way he was going to fit inside a pair of business trousers and go to work; secondly, he would probably not be able to drive the Volvo without causing himself grievous bodily harm with the steering wheel on the first corner.

He called the office to explain that he was too sick to come to work and decided to take a long, cold shower, despite the water restrictions. It had some effect but he still caught himself painfully in the fridge door when he was looking for strawberry yoghurt.

Furious, he grabbed the package containing the remaining Adhesive Wonders and flushed them down the toilet. He was watching Sky News, standing up, when he heard an enormous explosion upstairs. He raced up to the bathroom and saw with amazement that the Wonder Strips had enjoyed one last conversion.

The U-bend behind the toilet was now straight, the seat itself had been torn from its base, and there was water everywhere.

In sheer desperation, He called the plumber.

A SAD DISAPPEARANCE

According to Fox News, Ethel Crawford's aircraft had disappeared in the thick jungle of the Santa Maria Valley in Baratoga This small South American republic was renowned for its *centella sublime*, a potent national drink made from cactus juice and palm roots, but this was not the reason for Aunt Ethel's visit. The family knew that the old lady was on another of her eccentric excursions, this time looking for a species of butterfly, unknown to the scientific world but worshipped by the local Indians.

Some members of the family faced more important issues, such as mortgages or putting a kid through a private school, so they were delighted when, John Crawford, one of her nephews, took the initiative of inviting the family to his large home in Ashmeadow to discuss what action, if any, they should take.

John expressed the opinions of most of the family around the table.

"Bugger the butterflies, what about the money?"

Ethel Crawford had inherited vast amounts of money from great uncle Nicholas, founder of the Globe Providence Insurance Company, and the family was concerned that the old spinster might have wasted much of their inheritance on futile research 3of unknown wonders in inaccessible places.

"I asked her once what was left," Peter Appleton, another nephew, complained. "Her reply was not even polite!"

"The money I inherited is mine, great uncle wanted me to use it for my research," she had declared firmly. "You can keep your grimy noses and your greedy fingers out of my purse."

A few weeks ago, the news that she was going overseas and that the trip would take at least four months, was a delight for many members of the family. John Crawford had been pleased to tell his wife that for the next one hundred and twenty two days, when the doorbell rang '*La Cucaracha*', it would not announce the arrival of 'the old loony' with her large patchwork bag, her black hat covered in imitation cherries and her spiteful tongue.

The eccentric aunt had decided long ago that John's children were uncouth, sloppy, dirty, badly dressed, loud-mouthed and insolent. John was a man who accepted the twenty-first century for what it was, and he did not need Aunt Ethel to remind him of his children's shortcomings. Nevertheless, he secretly admired the old lady's courage and determination and had been proud to boast to close friends that his 'dear auntie' had bravely set out to find the elusive Golden Hummer, the only butterfly to fly backwards with its eyes closed.

Once the aeroplane accident had been confirmed, Trevor Sprocket, under-secretary for Foreign Relations and Trade Deficits and a close friend of John Crawford, had asked him if the Australian government should send a vice-consul to look for her. Although they had a surplus of junior diplomats at that time, John had declined the offer.

"The family has absolute faith in the in the government and the business community of Baratoga," he had lied. "We also believe that we should proudly celebrate her contribution to science and to devote the money she leaves behind her to the needy and the less fortunate."

He did not mention that among the 'needy and less fortunate' there were several nephews and nieces of the defunct explorer. He also overlooked the rumour that the wealthiest members of the Baratoga business community were drug traffickers and exporters of delicious young girls with big, big brown eyes, very popular in Spain as complacent housemaids.

After all, there had been no shortage of good advice for the now missing aunt at the last family Christmas luncheon.

"You do not realise the pleasures that a well-managed portfolio could provide," her sister Doris had told her. "Just imagine yourself with a comfortable home in Sutton Vale, filled with tasteful Italian furniture and a few oil paintings, with a magnificent view over the lake."

"Knitting, even with a cat on your knees, could have been a very soothing effect for the soul on a winter afternoon," the other sister, Mavis had added.

"And if you are interested in the flora and fauna of foreign lands, it would be far more comfortable and less dangerous to sit at home and watch some Attenborough DVD's on a six foot plasma," John Crawford himself had suggested. "When a volcano erupts in Indonesia or a freak wave destroys a couple of exotic islands, you simply send a small cheque to WorldVision, along with a card and a few kind words, naturally."

Ethel had snorted angrily.

"You sit in your pitiful little brick-veneers, drive around in your stupid cars, watch rubbish on television and ignore the wonders of the world around you," she shouted angrily. "My money is devoted to research and helping primitive civilisations, not to paying off a four-star rated fridge!"

"Some of us are not very wealthy," her sister Mavis pleaded." Generosity and help can start with your own family, you know."

"Don't be silly, "Aunt Ethel growled. "You waste money on futilities. Give me another glass of Chardonnay!"

John sighed. All eighteen members of the family had received the same Christmas present from Aunt Ethel this year, a book called 'Saving the Orang-utans in Borneo.' It was not exciting reading.

"When the 'old loony' comes home, she sits in her rocking chair in that draughty old house in Blaxford, reading National Geographic and preparing her next expedition," John lamented. "She's a founding member of those fruitcakes who call themselves the Questers of the Unknown World."

Mavis and Doris nodded sadly

"My roof is leaking again," Doris moaned. "She told me to call a plumber."

"My house hasn't had a coat of paint in twenty years," Mavis sighed.

John was still battling with those he called 'the fruitcakes'.

"They search the jungles looking for lost civilisations, politicians in exile, unknown fauna or abandoned Land Rovers", he joked.

Nobody laughed.

Oddly enough, the Questers approached the family a few weeks after Ethel's disappearance to invite them to meet Brother Lazarus who had served as a missionary in the Santa Maria Valley. The explorer's two sisters were appointed by the family to encounter the man of God.

"I'll take my tape recorder with me," Mavis decided.

"Good idea," John approved.

The appointment was in a roadside eatery full of tattooed truck drivers in blue singlets, on the road to Maverton Plains. The poor sisters were terrified by the blaring hard rock music and the overwhelming smell of burning fat, and when the owner pointed out Brother Lazarus sitting in a booth, Doris nearly fainted. He was well over six feet tall, with a shiny bald head and a long curly black beard. He wore a black leather waist coast and his left arm was tattooed with an image of the Virgin Mary sitting on a Harley Davidson. The words 'Riding with God' were on a scroll below the picture.

The two ladies sat down, at his gestured invitation, and Mavis introduced herself and her sister in a squeaky, trembling voice.

"I need breakfast", he muttered, and gestured to the waitress.

"We're not very hungry," Mavis whispered shyly. "We'll just have a cup of coffee."

He grunted and ordered the Harry Super Special with three mugs of coffee. Mavis was looking at a ketchup stained menu and pointed out to her sister the ingredients to the breakfast he had ordered: steak, lambs fry, sausages, two eggs, hash brown, mushrooms, chips, grilled tomatoes and baked beans.

"I'm a bit off my food at the moment," he explained, and the two sisters nodded sympathetically.

"You're Ethel's sisters?" he asked. There was almost a glimmer of gentleness in his eyes.

They nodded dumbly.

"Well, she's probably dead and I'll tell you why," he announced abruptly. "After breakfast."

Doris nodded and Mavis dabbed the corner of her left eye with a handkerchief. John had insisted that they show deep sadness at the loss of their sister and that they avoid above all any suggestion of loot, that is to say a heritage.

"The men of the Church have greedy hands," John had warned them wisely.

"And we are very poor," Mavis had added.

"I certainly can't afford to make donations," Doris had explained.

"Then you must be careful," John had concluded.

When the sumptuous breakfast arrived, Brother Lazarus began shovelling food into his mouth like a man who had not eaten for a week. Beans and ketchup were running down his leather waistcoat and Doris shuddered at such manners. The two sisters looked at one another and exchanged a cautious frown. The spectacle offered by a supposed man of the cloth was repugnant.

People around them were gradually leaving and the jukebox had fallen silent. Waitresses were clearing the tables and wiping down the Formica tops with greasy cloths. Brother Lazarus slurped down his mug of luke warm coffee and sat back with a deep sigh, patting his extended belly. Then he began to talk.

According to the missionary's theory, many of the plane's passengers would have died in the crash itself. Among the survivors, some would have succumbed to the venomous snakes or spiders that infested the valley. If the remaining living had waited too long, the smell of their perspiration could well have attracted the Wattabanga Dragons, carnivorous lizards over two metres long that lived in the jungle. This reptile only removed small pieces of flesh at each bite, as it liked to savour its food, so that humans that fell into its claws would have had ample time to prepare themselves for their reunion with the Creator. The thick canopy of trees would have muffled their screams of pain.

Mavis and Doris listened and sobbed into their lace handkerchiefs, imagining the agony their poor sister Ethel must have suffered. With a reassuring smile, the man of God pressed on, suggesting that a few may well have escaped all these dangers and reached the Kramanga River. Here, they would have met members of Kakakiki tribe who would have taken them back to a village for food and shelter. Feeling a little reassured, Mavis and Doris pulled clean handkerchiefs from their bags and smiled at one another bravely.

"Ethel was a good walker and a wonderful linguist," Doris suggested reassuringly.

"The Kakakiki people loved Europeans and considered them as a gift of their gods," Brother Lazarus explained. "Sister Paola, who is on mission there at the moment, sent me an Email a few days ago to announce the appearance of a 'white queen'.

Mavis and Doris exchanged glances.

"Could this be Ethel?" Doris asked.

Brother Lazarus shrugged his shoulders.

"Who knows? The Kakakiki have a habit of keeping their more tempting captives in large pens and of feeding them well, so that they would later become essential ingredients for a the traditional annual feast of fertility."

Doris shuddered when he added, eyes gleaming, that young Spanish nuns, roasted on a spit and served with sweet chilli sauce, corn on the cob and steamed yams, had been a traditional local delicacy since the sixteenth century, although the custom had been recently banned by UNESCO. He explained that he had lived among these Indians for several years. He had explored local vegetation, discovered new herbs and spices, and had started preparing new dishes, based very vaguely on a Nigela Lawson cookbook he had taken with him. The natives, suitably impressed with his skills, had allowed him to deliver Christ's message from the dining table rather than from inside the cooking pot.

"Ethel was quite handy in the kitchen," Mavis suggested shyly.

"Don't be silly, girl, Doris admonished her. "Her scrambled eggs were as thick as rice pudding!"

After that meeting, the contents of which were dutifully reported to the family by the two aunts, John rang Trevor Sprocket. He mentioned the story of the 'white queen' and Trevor suggested that it would not be wise to commit resources and funds on a search party for an appearance based on gossip. John agreed wholeheartedly and almost enthusiastically.

The family relaxed gradually. They felt some reassurance in believing that, in one form or another, their dear aunt had joined the Lord, and that her soul was at peace. As was her bank account, according to discreet enquiries made by John Crawford at the Bank of Melbourne.

One year and six months after her disappearance, Trevor Sprocket rang John to thank him for the donation to the Baratoga Orphans Christmas Fund and announced that the authorities of that country had declared his aunt officially dead. When John Crawford reunited the family for a Sunday barbecue to announce that the solicitor, Peter Flanagan, had invited the whole family to be present in his Ashmeadow offices the following Wednesday, when he would read her will, cheers broke out. John called for immediate silence and warned them that an appropriate gravity should be ensured during that meeting. Finally only six of them attended, including John himself, Mavis and Doris and three great nieces. The others were at home making wild guesses at what their share of the loot would be.

Peter Flanagan, who had the reputation of having the highest fees in regional Victoria, began to talk, and John Crawford tried not to imagine an invisible meter spinning madly. The solicitor reminded the family, slowly and expensively, of all the events that had preceded this meeting. He declared that any aircraft disaster is a sad event, but that when you are flying over the uncharted jungles of Baratoga in a clapped out Tupolev with a Samoan pilot, you are taking exceptional risks. He added that it had been impossible to identify the site of the crash from the air and local authorities had decided not to waste money and resources by undertaking a fruitless search for survivors. Under Baratogan law, three years must pass by before the death of the expedition's members could become official; however in this case the authorities had been more indulgent. John smiled proudly; his donation had not gone unnoticed. The solicitor also reminded them of the meeting between Mavis, Doris and Brother Lazarus.

Having recalled all these events during more than an hour, Mr Flanagan opened the will with an expensive flourish. Before reading their aunt's last wishes, he presented a document from the Baratogan Department of Forests, Archaeology and Iron Cooking Pots and invited them to acknowledge it as an official death certificate. It confirmed that the forest wardens believed that their aunt now existed as compost on the forest floor and it thanked the family for this unusual contribution to a World Heritage jungle. Chantal Chervet, a great niece and a staunch supporter of the Greens, sobbed into her recycled paper handkerchief as Mr Flanagan withdrew the will from the large brown envelope. It was an impressive document.

The first endowment was an amount of 16,000 dollars to provide the deceased with an appropriate tomb in a cemetery in Blaxford. However, as she had died in a dangerous jungle, a military aircraft would parachute a commemorative plaque into the forest close to the presumed site of the accident. No local funeral director was game to enter into the jungle itself.

There were gasps of surprise as the solicitor announced the total amount that Aunt Ethel had distributed among her heirs. She had not wasted her inheritance, as they had thought, but invested it carefully on international markets, and most of her descendants were going to inherit some handsome gifts. Mavis and Doris would be off the Centrelink pension and would be able to realise their dream, that of buying that modern unit they had dreamed of sharing in Midvale. Others were to receive cash and shares amounting to several million dollars. The small group left the solicitor's office, happy, stunned, and eager to share the good news with the other members of the family. Her acerbic criticism of their private lives and her frequent uninvited invasion of their homes were forgotten. They went their different ways, determined, for some, to enjoy their inheritance, for others to pay their debts, while all trying desperately to look contrite.

As the years passed, there were few communications between members of the family; wealthy people have so little time for the mundane, apart from exchanging cheap cards at Christmas. The greatest surprise of all came late in 2004 when the ABC's Foreign Correspondent sent three journalists with portable cameras deep into the Upper Wattabanga Valley. They discovered what they believed to be the world's largest marijuana plantation. The owner was known as the Great White Queen of Kakakiki.

John Crawford recognised her immediately from the blurred photos and rang Trevor Sprocket in the Department of Foreign Affairs and Trade Deficits who advised him that if the person seen was indeed Aunt Ethel, she had probably lost her memory, her marbles and her passport, in that order. In any case, diplomatic relations were temporarily suspended with the Republic of Baratoga, because of Australian Greens senator's interference in their internal affairs. John Crawford assured him that it was not important and the family did not wish to enter in contact with the Great White Queen, believing that it was not Aunt Ethel, and even if it was the dear aunt was probably quite happy where she was. All the heirs approved this philanthropic statement enthusiastically and a second and more generous contribution was sent to Bara toga's orphans.

The family is today reasonably sure that she will never return to Australia. Nevertheless, some of them are still dreading a visit from the 'old loony' with her carpetbag, her ugly hat and her acerbic tongue. Every time that the doorbell rings La Cucaracha, John Crawford's heart skips a beat.

THE SAD WAITER

Gaston Lagoutte was not a happy man. He was homesick and dreamt of his beloved Paris every night. He had discovered that his assumed knowledge of the English language was seriously tested in this strange land called Australia. Worse, today he was being driven to a meeting in a country town, on the wrong side of the road, and his driver was a tall, muscular blond man who appeared to be infuriated by what he was hearing on the van's radio.

Gaston listened carefully and tried to understand the debate that was being broadcast.

The new Green Senator, Reginald Oaktree, was adamant.

"There are those, and they are numerous, who question the usefulness of SPEED, the Society for the Promotion and Enjoyment of Ethnic Diversity," he declared emphatically to the eight other senators who had just dragged themselves back from lunch. "Its benefactor, Henry Waggle, is one of those impossible gentlemen who have too much influence among those who need to feel secure in their incompetent management of national affairs."

Senator Fred Whistle, the proud and sole representative of the Family Protection Party, jumped to his feet to agree.

"These newcomers should not be allowed to inflict their boring philosophies on those who prefer a one-day cricket match or a quiet read of the Christian Chronicle," he added.

Senator Wiseman, an independent observer on the Unexplained Expenses Commission, was even more virulent.

"Considering the amount of money the government seems to throw at this imbecile Waggle and his ridiculous ideas," he intervened, "Would not the funds be more usefully spent by sending him on a fact-finding mission to Lower Borneo?"

"Do we need facts from Lower Borneo?" the petulant National Party Senator, Josephine Harvester asked.

"We will only know if he spends a couple of years there looking for them," an exasperated Senator Wiseman retorted.

With a sigh, Henry Waggle, Gaston's host and driver, turned off the radio in his van and pulled into the kerb. For Gaston, Mr Waggle was a very important man who was going to present his distinguished French visitor to an august assembly of citizens of Blaxford. Rude people shouting at one another over the airwaves should not disturb his guest.

Despite persistent criticism and lack of popularity, Henry Waggle's SPEED and his itinerant program of explaining the advantages of multicultural immigration was a success. No political party was prepared to declare that multiculturism was dead, although nationalistic agitators were claiming that integration was the only solution. His secret was his understanding of politics and his agility in playing opposing ideologies against one another. He presented his philosophy almost always to a large audience, the packed auditorium often filled by residents from aged care centres, Centrelink referees, teenagers on conversion programs, Salvation Army *protégés*, abandoned wives, would-be writers seeking inspiration, free-lance journalists and actors with nothing else to do. He received generous and conscience-stricken funding from exotic programmes most of which you and I had never heard of.

An almost terrified Gaston Lagoutte was whisked on to the stage and placed on a chair at a long table, facing an audience of several hundred. Henry Waggle, at his side, leaned over and whispered into his ear.

"Don't worry", he told him." I will do all the talking, you just have to nod and smile. It's very easy."

When feet had stopped shuffling, throats had stopped clearing and chairs were no longer scraping the wooden floor, Henry Waggle rose to his feet, thanked his audience and launched himself into the introduction of Gaston Lagoutte, his neighbour, another fine example of ethnic and cultural diversity.

"Gaston is an emblem of Paris", he told the public, as an introduction. "When you visit Paris, what do you remember? Of course, the Eiffel Tower, the Louvre museum, Pigalle, the boulevards and avenues, the pretty girls, the honking motor cars. But I bet that millions of visitors will also remember the waiters in the cafés and brasseries."

To his delight, an elderly gentleman shouted "Hear, hear' with gusto.

"For over forty years," Henry continued, "Gaston Lagoutte was a waiter in Paris and you will have seen hundreds and hundreds of men who looked just like him. Even today, the *garçons de café*, with their black waistcoats and trousers, white shirts and black bow ties, are the life and soul of the city; more important than the policemen and the whores, so they claim. Without them, Paris would be as dull and as boring as Adelaide!"

Several people laughed. Henry knew that to hold his public's attention, an occasional joke was important.

He continued to explain that for Gaston and his colleagues, tips are everything! Some waiters actually paid for the privilege of serving a group of tables in the reputed cafés on the grand avenues of the capital, and for them the 'service' or tip, had to offer a generous return on their investment. Others worked in the nice cafés where they paid no entry fee but earned no salary, living, like the others, only on the tips they earned. The others were in the popular cafés where they earned a modest wage and frugal tips. Gaston was of the latter category, and he worked in the *Café Java* that is not far from the Eiffel Tower and very close to the Australian Embassy.

Henry could see the expressions of surprise on the faces of some members of the public. He could also feel that, by his side, Gaston was beginning to relax and even smile.

"Gaston was born in Paris, although his parents came from the country, a little village in Normandy where he used to have a few uncles and aunts," Henry explained. "He visited them two or three times, for holidays, funerals of christenings. He never stayed for a long time in Normandy because he did not like the countryside with its cows, its old men in clogs, and its women in ugly flowered dresses."

Among the spectators a few middle-aged ladies in floral dresses and Akoubra hats frowned and shuffled their feet. Henry pressed on.

"In the *café* where Gaston worked, they sold provincial menus. Their customers enjoyed some of the best recipes from Normandy, Lyon, Brittany or Provence. They served wines from Bordeaux, Burgundy and Alsace, as well as champagne and cognac. In his *café*, customers enjoyed the best of French gastronomy without having to put up with what they saw as a boring rural life."

It became pretty obvious that Gaston was very much a city man.

"There were three areas of work in their *café:* the kitchen, where the food was prepared; the bar, that sold drinks, lottery tickets and cigarettes; and the brasserie, with its dining room and adjoining footpath, where they served the meals," Henry explained. "It was called the *Café Java* because the previous owner travelled to the Dutch East Indies many years ago from where he brought back a Javanese princess who became his wife. There is a painting of the beautiful lady of Java, barely clothed, in the bar of the café. The boss says that if a client touches a bare brown breast, on the painting of course, it brings luck, and the state of the picture shows that many visitors have sought fortune within its walls."

The spectators were beginning to enjoy the presentation and the story of the Javanese princess and provoked some raucous giggles.

"Gaston had never travelled far or often," Henry explained. "He believed that travel was not necessary, because he lived in Paris, capital of the universe. He lived most of his adult life in a comfortable flat that he rented on the fourth floor of a nice building. His neighbours were a Polish prostitute, a Hungarian fortune teller, an American artist, two lesbian schoolteachers from Marseilles, Susanne the beautiful hairdresser from Lyon, two public servants, a Vietnamese baker, and an Algerian family that ran a little grocery shop around the corner. The whole world was on his doorstep."

"Sounds like Footscray," one spectator called out.

"Can't be. No drunks, no empty beer cans on the footpath!" another spectator commented, provoking some hearty laughter.

"When he first came to work in the *Café Java,* just before the war, Gaston was employed in the kitchen where his job was to wash saucepans and dishes, to suffer the bursts of rage of the cook and to duck when he threw knives or fry pans at his staff. Later, he moved on to the bar where he served drinks, coffee and cigarettes."

Henry paused for a few seconds, listening to the murmured comments, before continuing.

"Gaston admits that he was not active in the Resistance. When the dreaded *Boches* invaded France and Pétain signed an armistice, the waiters of Paris undertook a passive, discreet form of Resistance. He believes that de Gaulle must have been very proud, although historians have overlooked their battle against the hated invader. They did not blow up trains or attack German forces in the mountains. Their war was bacterial: every time a hated German soldier ordered a coffee, they spat in the cup before taking it out to him."

This statement provoked some very hearty laughter and Gaston grinned happily.

"When the Germans left," Henry added, "Parisians shaved the heads of their abandoned girlfriends, bought black-market cigarettes from the Americans, got the good wine out from under the cellar floor and went back to normal life. Gaston's café would open at six thirty in the morning and some of its customers would be there by seven for their traditional breakfast: a glass of white wine and a hard-boiled egg. Coffee drinkers would come in all through the day and when they took away the ashtrays away to stop them smoking at the bar, in the eighties, they just threw their butts on the floor. Parisians are proud people and do not take orders from politicians and policemen."

Henry could feel that the disparate public was warming to his description of life in a Parisian café. Even Gaston Lagoutte was feeling the growing enthusiasm in the room, and began to wave to certain spectators.

"They sold lottery and scratch tickets all day long," Henry explained. "In 1968, when Paris was in the middle of a revolt, Georges, the fishmonger, Gaston's best friend, won eighteen million francs, sold his shop and bought a big house on the coast in Brittany. Two years later, he came back; the quiet and the solitude were driving him crazy. All he heard all day was the crash of the waves and the wind and the rain rattling his shutters. Gaston saw his friend's return as a great victory, and Georges moved into a comfortable flat above a shop selling horse meat and his bedroom window looks over the street. Through the night, he hears the drunks leaving the bars, the alarms going off as they bump into cars parked on the footpath, the coaches picking up tourists at three in the morning to take them to Nice and the prostitutes discussing performance indicators with their clients. At dawn, the trucks come through emptying bins or washing the gutters, and then the shutters go up on the shop fronts and George can get out of bed, bleary-eyed, to tackle his first cup of coffee. George is a happy man, once again, and Gaston misses him badly."

This picturesque description of the less pretty aspect of life in Paris surprised many of the audience. Some were now leaning forward, sitting on the edge of their seats.

"Gaston worked long enough in the bar to realise that the *café* was the social hub of his district," Henry explained. "Then, in 1988, he moved to the brasserie to become a waiter. Paris is not Rome. He did not stand in front of the *café* to persuade people to come and eat there, boasting the merits of their menu. Most of their customers were regulars and when new patrons arrived, like the other the waiters, Gaston treated them with caution. He would flick an imaginary speck of dust from a chair with his tea towel and would sit them at the worst place outside, on the footpath at a table close to the traffic lights where they could breathe in the petrol and diesel fumes while drinking their *apéritif.* This was the test of their loyalty, perseverance and determination."

There was another spontaneous interruption of laughter. The public was warming to this shy little Frenchman sitting behind the table on the stage.

"If they came back again, Gaston would notice, inwardly pleased, but pretend not to recognise them. They still got a table outside, but further away from the exhaust fumes. They still got the grease-stained menu, and he still did not tell them about the *plat du jour,* in other words what is fresh today rather than heated-up leftovers. They had to learn loyalty the hard way. After four or five visits, he would recognise them, officially, with a terse '*bonjour monsieur*' or '*bonjour madame*', the faintest hint of a smile and a suggestion that they might be more comfortable inside. Now, for the first time, he would allow them to look at the menu of the day on the blackboard, and he might suggest a nice little wine that the owner has just received from his brother-in-law, winegrower in *Beaujolais*."

Some members of the audience were now whispering among themselves, marvelling at the gradual 'promotion' of a café customer.

"They gradually became regular customers," Henry explained. "People who learned that his name was Gaston, and that if they want good service they should look out for him and not forget his tip. They were among the chosen few, those who would be making a steady contribution to his retirement fund."

There was more laughter and Gaston was nodding eagerly. Henry pursued his story.

"Our friend had many regular customers: hairdressers, sales representatives, girls from shops or insurance companies, lawyers, bank employees, taxi drivers or pimps. He told me about Monsieur *Pascal* who once worked at the nearby Australian Embassy, and who ordered sausages, mash and Belgian beer every day. *Madame Gisèle* ran a smart boutique and often ate there with her lover, *Monsieur Serge* who owned a local bookshop. *Monsieur Albert* and *Madame Claudine*, who owned a cheese shop just down the street, lunched in his café every weekday for more than ten years."

There were people in the room smiling and nodding enthusiastically, encouraging the orator to continue this passionate story. Henry pressed on.

"Gaston Lagoutte's very best customers were those he had known for many years. He greeted them with a big smile and a hearty '*Bonjour, Monsieur Francois*' or '*Bonjour Madame Cécile*'. When they sat at the table at the back of the room, where it is warmer and quieter, he used to tell them that the *aperitif* was on the house and perhaps whisper in their ear that the pork chops were not the best that day but the *couscous* was excellent. When other diners heard him greet certain visitors loudly by their name, they looked up. They realised that these were important people they probably should recognise. *Monsieur Francois* and *Madame Cécile* walked towards their table proudly, looking ahead, shoulders back, nose raised. They were very respectable: they were his most cherished customers."

Gaston was quite carried away by the enthusiasm he felt in the room for his story. He stood up and flicked imaginary dust from the conference table with an imaginary duster. The round of laughter and applause that greeted this for this Manuel-like gesture interrupted the speaker momentarily.

"They also had tourists," Henry told them, grinning with delight. "Gaston enjoyed studying foreign women, telling himself how lucky he was to be a Parisian. He found the English, Dutch and German women inelegant and often bulky, their Italians and Spanish counterparts dark and exciting and he loved the little Japanese girls, who knew only a few words of French but who would giggle hopelessly at everything he said. Nevertheless, he was a patriot. His sentimental life was limited to a night of fantasy, every Saturday, with Suzanne, a true French beauty, the hairdresser who lived next door. Her husband spent every weekend with his cousins in *Rouen,* or so he said. There is a French expression that says that when the cat is out the mice dance. Susanne and Gaston danced often."

There were a few frowns from the ladies in floral dresses and Akoubra hats, but also some hearty laughter. Here was a typical Frenchman, as they imagined them. Gaston was now wearing an irrepressible grin and Henry could hardly hide his delight with the positive and encouraging reaction of an enthusiastic public. He pursued the story happily.

"Saturday was also market day, and the stalls would appear under the viaduct that carries the metro through the district. This was where Gaston bought his meat, poultry, game and vegetables for the week. He loved wandering between the stalls, listening to the vendors boasting their products, watching the migrants from Eastern Europe selling their wares, smelling the herbs and spices from Italy, Arabia and Asia. It seemed that his destiny was engraved in gold on the pavement in front of the *Café Java*. Then disaster struck!"

The public was silent, holding its breath. Gaston, realising that the speaker had reached the sad moment of his life, took on a solemn look. Henry Waggle lowered his voice, becoming more sober. He took on an almost conspiratorial tone.

"Gaston's employer sold the *Café Java*. The building was demolished and he believes that it is now the site of a sushi bar, employing a throng of pseudo-Japanese waitresses. His lovely Suzanne ran away to Corsica, leaving her husband and her lover, to live with an Italian greengrocer. To celebrate her departure her husband paid Gaston an unfriendly visit. He broke his nose and the mirror in his hallway. With no money and no job, Gaston regretfully accepted the hospitality of a cousin in Ashmeadow, He did not realise that Australia was so far away from his beloved Paris. Bravely, he found himself a job in the local service station."

One lady in a floral dress had removed her Akoubra and was sobbing uncontrollably in her handkerchief.

"So much talent wasted," Henry commented sadly. "Gaston tells me that when he returns at night to his small bedroom in his cousin's house, he closes his eyes and floats back to Paris. Edith Piaf sings him to sleep, and he dreams of pretty girls, honking taxis and the rumble of the Métro. *Monsieur Francois* and *Madame Cécile* visit him every night in his dreams, and he tells them that today the Beef *Bourguigon* is excellent and that the boss has just bought a few cases of *Côtes du Rhone* that will accompany the tender and tasteful dish excellently. And that is all I can tell you about the life of Gaston. Are there any questions?"

Immediately, a woman at the back of the hall stood up and was handed a microphone.

Bernadette explained her restaurant *Chez Victor* in Ashmeadow and how she offered a French menu based on old cookbooks inherited from her mother.

"Gaston, I need a man to look after the clients, to explain the dishes, to suggest the wines, to make them feel as if they are really in a French restaurant. Would you like to work with me?"

There was a moment of stunned silence. Then a lady let out a great cheer and tossed her Akoubra hat into the air. As Bernadette and Gaston fell into one another's arms, hugging one another in a typical French way of acknowledging a workplace agreement, a delighted crowd whistled and clapped.

A few months later, Henry Waggle was invited to dine at the *Chez Victor* restaurant. It was packed and Gaston Lagoutte, new partner in the business, thanks to a discreet investment from a savings fund in Luxembourg, was delighted.

"We will be opening a second restaurant in Blaxford, Bernadette explained. "Gaston has a friend who was chef in the café where he worked; he will be joining us to run the kitchen."

Gaston interrupted.

"I 'ave just receeved a letteur from Monsieur Francois and Madame Cécile,": he explained excitedly, with his inimitable French accent "They are coamin' to Austraalia on 'oliday and will be visiting me next monse."

BRIGITTE MURPHY'S VISION

There are two small towns in our region with very different cultural backgrounds and conflicting philosophies: they are the communities of Midvale and Newbridge.

The inhabitants of Midvale are mostly of rough English stock, many the descendants of the poor and unemployed dragged from the gutters of eighteenth century London. It has four pubs but not one had a beer garden. The most popular was the Lion's Head, near the abattoir and many a village girl had lost her innocence on one of the benches surrounding the bottle-strewn car park, on a sultry Friday summer night.

The village of Newbridge lies further south, close to the babbling source of the Kathleen River. It is a peaceful and pious community and premarital pregnancy is as rare as a bacon sandwich at a rabbi's wedding. There are three pubs in Newbridge: the Celtic Arms, the Green Man and O'Reilly's. They all have saloon bars with deep pile carpet, darts boards, log fires and eighteen varieties of Irish whiskey. All the inhabitants are the God-fearing descendants of three honourable families from County Cork that had fled the potato famine and the English landowners.

These first settlers in Newbridge had been Sean and Mary Kelly, Allin and Molly Murphy and Paddy and Colleen O'Neill. Mary had chosen the name of the village, settled on land bought with money offered by distant cousins in America. Today's inhabitants are the descendants of those settlers.

The Kelly family set up a farm and a business that later produced the finest bacon and pork sausages in the land. The Kelly sausage has won the prize for the best in Country Victoria eight times. In fact, according to a popular rumour, an Elstenwick second hand car dealer had invited all his friends for a Kelly pork sausage barbecue the day his wife walked out on him to run away with a hairdresser called Gloria.

Allin Murphy had bred some of the greatest racehorses in the land, and his most famous champion, Erin Boy, now stands stuffed in a regional museum. Over his head is a banner that declares '*Ni Dhénfaah An Saol Capall Rása D'Asal', which* in the old language tells you that the world will never breed a racehorse from a donkey. Donkeys only produce bookmakers, as we all know.

The O'Neill family originally farmed potatoes, what else, but later began producing all manner of foreign vegetables like courgette and aubergine. It was on their land that Paddy's daughter, Teagan, first discovered the spring. It came from far, far down in the Earth, maybe from Ireland itself if the truth were known. They bottled that water and although Teagan believed that it was a gift from Our Gracious Mother and would only heal the true believers, even heathens and Protestants swore that it cured their rheumatism and gout.

The three families have always guarded the village for themselves and never sold land to newcomers. Nevertheless, it has grown and prospered, and their children married their children and their grandchildren married their grandchildren. This was why they all have the same fat noses, the same squinty eyes and the same wide ears. They begat incessantly in the Lord's name, begetting together, letting no foreigner come among them, finally producing a genetic characteristic that the people in Midvale rudely called the Newbridge Squint.

The only unusual person in the village was Brigitte Murphy. Old Father Brandon, whose eyesight was poorly, pointed her out to Father O'Connell during the last Mass he was to celebrate in the village.

"Look around you, Cletus O'Connell," he whispered as they called the congregation to their feet. "They've all got the fat nose of the Kelly's, or the little squinty eyes of the Murphy's or the big ears of the O'Neill's. But not little Brigitte."

The young priest agreed. When Brigitte walked down the main street, skirt swaying on her ample hips, firm breasts bouncing in her starched blouse, Father O'Connell almost forgot his vows of chastity. He was surely not the only one in the village to notice how much she looked like Jack Anderson, a Protestant from Midvale. Jack, a handsome man with twinkling blue eyes, had been a stable hand with the Murphy family for nigh on twenty years. Brigitte Murphy's mother never came to confession, which was such a pity. Priests love gossip, so they say.

The lack of new migrants was beginning to stifle the village. The pig farm, the sausage factory, the racehorse stable and the market gardens were fine, but the people of Newbridge needed to create new jobs. Allin Murphy had the idea of setting up a tourist information centre which would encourage visitors to see the horses train, to taste the bacon and the waters of the magic spring and watch the beautiful young step dancers. It was a difficult task and it was at that moment that the Almighty intervened.

The bishop's car broke down one day a few hundred yards from Newbridge and ended up in O'Neill's Garage. The man of God thought that it was only a problem with a fan belt, but the Lord moves in mysterious ways, even with motor vehicles, and Michael O'Neill quickly discovered that the brakes were worn, that the steering was loose and that the shock absorbers were banging as if the devil himself was hoping to shake the poor bishop to death. Patricia Kelly whispered to Father O'Connell that perhaps Michael had 'created' some of the problems.

"*Ara be Whist!*" He told her. "Why, if that little fan belt had not broken near our little community, we might well have lost our dear bishop today. Michael attends Mass every Sunday, so we know that the Lord guides his adjustable spanner."

His Worship was so grateful that he talked about Newbridge during sermon in the Cathedral the following Sunday and the week after local television stations sent brazen blondes with tight pullovers accompanied by pushy cameramen with ear rings and faded jeans to interview its residents. Gradually, every weekend, the streets of Newbridge filled with painted women, loud men and badly behaved children, all seeking the joys of the Newbridge sausage, its vegetables and its water. Father O'Connell thanked the Lord for His Patience when they even invaded the Church, taking photos during the sermon, standing up when he told them to kneel, sitting down when he told them to stand, but singing with such fervour that it was as if the eyes and ears of the Almighty were upon them.

Scots, Indians, Greeks, Poles and Maoris prayed in the Church, and Saint Patrick was so pleased that he whispered to Aileen Kelly in her dreams that the heathens could finance the repairs of the Church roof. Allin Murphy placed a sign in front of the Church, announcing two Masses every Sunday morning, attendance costing ten dollars per person for the front pews and five dollars elsewhere. The Bishop was delighted. He was just back from a marketing seminar in Rome, and knew that this was the new way, and that marketing consultants like Allin Murphy, were all the rage in the Vatican.

Now, at the end of each Mass, the priest offered a prayer for the Carlton Football Club, boasted the cleansing merits of the spring waters and underlined the well-being provided by the good old Irish breakfast served at the Celtic Arms Hotel. This, his grace had explained, was sponsorship, and it pleased the Lord.

Not surprisingly, during their visits to the region, the good people of Melbourne also discovered Midvale, the other small town, nowadays filled with all manner of heathens: Methodists, Presbyterians, Lesbians, Uniting Protestants, Hells Angels, Avon representatives and Krishna devotees thronged its streets. With the invasion came the developers and old houses fell down, new mansions grew out of the rubble, four-wheel drive monsters filled the streets and new shops appeared everywhere.

Allin Murphy set up a bus service between the two towns. Very soon, Newbridge women with head scarves, sunglasses and high heel shoes began shopping in the neighbouring town. Father O'Connell met Patricia Kelly at the Coles express checkout twice in the same week. But he also discovered that there were shops in Midvale devoted to the strange customs. Some sold bronze sculptures and posters of idols with eight arms, and candles of many colours and shapes. Others offered organic cabbage, apples, turnips and walnuts. There were shops selling raspberry wine and gooseberry honey, essential oils, sausages made from soya bean flour, dandelion salad and bread baked according to Swedish, Zulu or Nepalese traditions.

Ross O'Neill met Father O'Connell in the main street there one morning and Ross nudged the priest as they passed two well-built ladies with paratrooper-style haircuts, cowboy boots and pink fluorescent earrings.

"The place is full of 'em," Ross explained. "Bean flickers or carpet munchers, whatever you want to call them. It's like Sodom and Begorrah, I'm telling you, and it's a disgrace to see such goings on!"

When the good priest got home, he rang the bishop and asked what 'bean flickers' and 'carpet munchers' might be. The bishop laughed.

"That'll be the ladies who practise homosexual activities together, lesbians I think the English call them. There are those who want to see Our Church employ female priests. Can you imagine what would be going on behind the altar if we did that?"

The good priest was horrified. He knew about the men of the cloth who had brought shame upon the Church, but he also knew that the arrival of 'bean flickers' would be far worse! Nevertheless, the traders of Midvale were drawing the Melbourne credit card away from Newbridge.

It was at that opportune moment that Brigitte Murphy met Our Lady at the spring. Brigitte often visited Murphy's Knob, the little hill above the source, and some suggested that she tasted the wild mushrooms that grew there. When she came down to the village, some evenings, she would have a strange look in her eyes, and she would stagger and mumble to herself, a little like Shamus O'Neill after too many ales at the Celtic Arms.

That particular evening she was pale, she was shaking, and she was saying "Mary, Mary, Mary' over and over again. Her father, Allin, called Father O'Connell and she told him, sobbing, that the Blessed Virgin, face a-shining, had come to her and told her that the water in the spring had truly miraculous properties. She said it could cure hepatitis B, measles, infidelity, Protestantism, blocked kidneys, obesity and the addiction to the poker machines. The poor priest, shaken to his marrow, left their house in deep thought.

He knew that Brigitte's mother, Maeve, had been to Lourdes last year and had come back amazed by the miracles, and the number of tourists she had seen there. Had she whispered the idea of the 'miracles' to her daughter? Extraordinary cures were a Godsend for the Church, to be sure, but non-believers would be waiting to pounce. The good priest feared that Allin Murphy might well seize the opportunity to promote the new wonders recklessly and without first consulting the Almighty in prayer.

How right he was. Within a few days, the Newbridge Office of Tourism was selling small wax statuettes of Brigitte, as well as photos showing a vague holistic face appearing between stark trees. Every night, crowds gathered on the side of the hill to gasp and chatter as heavenly lights flickered in the sky. Some heard voices.

Father O'Connell was no fool. He knew about laser guns, MP3's, laptops and computerised photo management programs and he knew that Allin's brother, Dorian was a magician in new technologies. Finally, and after many prayers and much hesitation, the good priest jumped on his Matchless motorbike and went to see the bishop He was greeted by a cheerful "*Dia is Muira duit*", an old Irish welcome hoping that God and Mary were with him.

"I think they are," he told the bishop. "Well, Mary is, at least."

Then he explained the machinations developing in Newbridge. The wise bishop patted his knee, making him jump nervously, and gazed at him very solemnly.

"Would you be after challenging the Almighty's decisions?" he asked him. "Do you know that He is keeping up with new marketing strategies much faster than you, my poor Cletus? Would you not be looking at a new organ for the Church next year? You know, one of those wonderful Japanese devices so great that they sing the Lord's praise without human intervention. If you want a miracle, then here is one that would bring tears to your eyes."

Father O'Connell acknowledged hesitantly that new technology could be a blessing. The bishop's eyes twinkled.

"Allin Murphy tells me that he believes that the parish priest might like to get around visiting his parishioners in a Green Hyundai I30 with air conditioning, like the ones Father O'Daly drives in Melbourne. Your motorbike could go to a museum, as a donation, if you will. And if the worshippers keep coming to see Brigitte you will have more money to succour the old, the weak and the poor in your community. Would that not be fine work for the Lord?"

Father O'Connell agreed reluctantly that it would be, indeed, very fine work for the Almighty. Bravely, he decided to call the bishop by his first name.

"You know, Neil, it worries me that they say the face of Our Lady, when it appears very mistily through the trees, looks just a little like that actress woman, Cate Blanchett."

Neil clapped his hands in glee.

"That lovely girl with the red hair? She is a real child of Erin, for certain. She has been surely blessed by the Lord to have such talent."

Father O'Connell decided that His Holiness was a man who saw good everywhere, not an old cynical like himself. He did not like apparitions based on video clips of famous stars.

Before the doubting priest left, the bishop slipped a bottle of fine Tasmanian Merlot into his satchel, patted him on the shoulder and wished him a safe return.

"Peace and prosperity be upon you and your flock," he told him, hoping that the priest would not stir the hornet's nest. As he left, the priest noticed that there were marvellous odours coming from the kitchen, and he guessed that young Betty O'Hara would be spoiling his holiness again tonight. Such a pretty wrench, too!

Nuait is gann é an bea is ea fial é roinnt', he thought to himself, while doubting whether the bishop would agree that when food is scarce it is generous to share. As he kicked the starter, he asked God for forgiveness for having unholy thoughts about the bishop's companion, about Brigitte Murphy and about spontaneous appearances and switched on the headlight. So be it, he told himself. He would return to Newbridge to market God's services to believers and non-believers alike, with the help of Allin Murphy.

That night, when all the inhabitants of the village were asleep, he climbed Murphy's Knob and on a small patch of grass, he knelt down and asked for Our Lady's blessing. He had only pronounced a few words when there was a terrible explosion and a flash of light. He saw a silhouette he thought he recognised, and he crossed himself in fear.

"Cletus O'Connell, you are a hypocrite," a female voice hissed. "You come praying to me, yet you do not believe in the work I am doing here. Would you not like to see a Bunnings and a Shell Service Station in this village, and a catholic primary school, perhaps we could call it Saint Brigitte of the Spring, overflowing with Apple computers?"

He attempted to babble contrite apologies but no man is a match for an angry woman, above all this one.

"If you do not believe, then you are not a true servant of God!" the silhouette shouted at the terrified priest.

Then she disappeared, and he fell flat on the ground, wondering if he was going mad or if he was the witness of a terrible hoax that served the interests of an ambitious community. The villagers, alerted by Allin Murphy and his grinning daughter, found their beloved priest on the ground, foaming at the mouth and babbling about plots and gunpowder, and they were very concerned about the good man's health. There was a red circle on his forehead and he shouted warnings against lust, greed, envy, pride, budget deficits and false messengers. Allin's brother took several photos and quickly collected all the material that he had left lying around that afternoon.

When the bishop saw the photos and heard the reports, he transferred Father O'Connell to quieter pastoral duties in a nursing home for the weak and the aged. Because Midvale was suddenly without a priest, he had to employ a young backpacker from Ireland to fill the gap, a lad who had done six months in a seminary and who had been working for the last year as a waiter in the Celtic Arms Hotel.

The routine reports the new priest brought to the bishop, concerning the holy apparitions, the fervent masses of new Christians and gratifying surpluses of the sacred treasury, brought great hope of pastoral promotion.

He could only hope that the Murphy family could keep their mouths shut.

FAMILY BUSINESS

Jack Ingham left Blaxford in 2004 to move to England with his family because his employer, Global Providence Insurance, wanted to set up a funeral insurance plan in the United Kingdom. As Jack had migrated to Australia some twelve years ago from England, with his French wife, Denise, he seemed to be the obvious choice. Daniel, his son, adapted quite quickly to his new life.

In 2010, Denise's aunt Gisele died suddenly of a heart attack, luckily before taking out funeral insurance. Her death put an end to a family feud of which Daniel had been an intermittent witness, and which he had secretly enjoyed. His mother, Denise, insisted that they all attend the funeral, to be held in her home village in Normandy, France. Jack believed that France had offered him two great pleasures: his wife, and good food. And for these reasons only, he accepted her decision. As they crossed a grey and very choppy Channel, Denise announced that the grey skies were mourning this sad departure and Jack asked if they would have the time to have dinner in *Le Coq Heureux*[11], his favourite restaurant in Normandy. Denise shrugged her shoulders angrily.

---

[11] The Happy Cockerel

"You are a Philistine," she announced angrily.

"Not true, I was born in Middlesex," he protested, with a twinkle in his eye.

It was all part of a game. Daniel's mother, was French and loved to deal with every event with what she saw as appropriate Gallic emotion. His father had adopted a healthy Australian cynicism and thought that a little humour was a good remedy for most problems.

There were about three dozen members of the French family at the ceremony; all were dressed in black although none of them appeared terribly overcome with sorrow. After the burial they all went to a local restaurant for the wake, not *Le Coq Heureux,* but Jack was not too disappointed.

"Better than burnt beef and three soggy veggies," he whispered to his son with a wink while checking the menu. Daniel knew he was talking about English grandmother's cooking.

They were very surprised to see great aunt Charlotte, Gisele's sister and worst enemy, sobbing over her plate of scallops a la crème, and almost choking with grief into her glass of white wine. Daniel whispered to his mother that he had counted that it was her fourth glass and she frowned angrily at him.

Jack had finished his scallops with gusto and was now enthusiastically tackling a hare stew baked in cider and accompanied by wild mushrooms, carrots and fresh cream. He was dribbling a fair amount of the delicious sauce down his shirt-front, but luckily his wife had not noticed. She was toying sadly with a peppered steak, and watching her aunt from the corner of her eye. When Charlotte asked loudly for a refill, Denise stood up and worked her way around the table towards the distressed aunt. When she finally reached her, she put her arm around her shoulder, hugged her, and reminded her gently that she had squabbled with her sister all her life.

"I know", sobbed Charlotte. "But I will miss her so!"

And then she added in a whisper.

"She died first just to spite me. Everyone knew that my heart condition was far worse than hers!"

Denise looked at her son and shrugged.

The Inghams were a happy family. Of course, the parents had occasional squabbles but Daniel knew that, as the French say, *la nuit porte conseil.* It means that good advice arrives during the night, and when the lights were out. After a family squabble, Daniel tucked himself under his duvet and waited for the armistice negotiations with bated breath. He would hear his father's deep voice murmuring sweet things, then his mother's giggle, and then the old four poster bed would begin to creak and he could go to sleep, knowing that peace had returned to the household.

The greatest threat to family happiness were the two aunts, Charlotte and Gisele, who came to visit in August every other year, delighted to see their niece back from that dreadful land at the other end of the world. The Ingham's small, elegant little English home was racked by screams and shouts as they abused one another in French. Daniel knew that the constant bickering put their cat, Winston, off his food. Denise had insisted on talking to her son in French at home, and thanks to his acquired linguistic skills he could follow the debate quite easily. His mother would go for long walks to leave the two enemies alone to shout abuse at one another, and he would hide behind a half-open door to listen and grin happily. His father would flee to the attic and hide, playing Pink Floyd very, very loudly to drown out the noise of the battle.

Daniel remembered a fight one Tuesday afternoon in 2008 very vividly.

"I see your lazy husband is not here again," Aunt Charlotte had screamed at her sister.

"You know he has a bad back and cannot travel," Aunt Gisele had replied. "Anyway, he says the sight of your ugly face makes him feel sick."

Aunt Gisele had laughed hysterically.

"It's the sight of work that makes him sick. How long is it since he last had a job, twenty years?"

Aunt Charlotte had stood firm, red-faced, fists clenched on ample hips.

"You know that he fell of a ladder when he was painting a ceiling in a large manor," she had shouted, spittle flying in the rays of sunlight coming through the French windows. "He is incapacitated."

Aunty Gisele wagged a threatening finger at her sister.

"The lazy sod was *born* incapacitated," she had screamed back. "Any way he didn't fall off the ladder, he jumped. He's been living off work accident insurance ever since."

Aunt Charlotte had become very pale but seemed to calm herself.

"If we want to talk about lazy scroungers, how is your Emile going?" she had asked with a bitter laugh. "Still wearing out the seats of his pants?"

"My husband is a respected public servant," Aunt Gisele had replied proudly. "A reputed public transport co-ordinator."

Aunt Charlotte had slapped her thigh with glee.

"He sells tickets in a rural railway station that sees only four trains a day," she had claimed. "The only day he gets his backside off the chair is when the union calls a strike."

The two aunts were now less than a metre apart at that moment and Denise stepped in through the French windows to move between them to prevent physical violence.

"Stop it, the two of you," she had snapped. "You're worse than spoilt kids!"

Aunt Gisele had turned around and walked out into the garden. Aunt Charlotte had dumped herself in an overstuffed armchair, pulled her reading glasses out of her apron pocket and began to read the local newspaper. Daniel grinned because he knew she could not read a word of English.

Today, he knew those days were now over. One of the protagonists had left them.

As the family sat on the train on the way back to Calais, his father snored and his mother took off her hat and settled back in her seat with a tired sigh. As Daniel watched the night sky flashing past through the train window, his mother began to explain the feud between the two sisters. It was simply a case of sister jealousy, each aspiring for the affection of a cold-hearted mother. She said that both carried physical and psychological scars from disputes during their younger years. She told him that this was why they spent most of the holiday with them shouting abuse at one another. Daniel asked why they came to visit at the same time if they did not like one another and she said it was because it offered the only opportunity to affront one another on neutral ground. Here, in France, since Charlotte's marriage, they never met and neither had attended the other's wedding.

It was a rough crossing back to England. Jack was sick and Denise told him that it was God punishing him for eating like a pig at the restaurant. Daniel sat out on deck, the collar of his coat pulled up around his ears, the wind whistling through his hair, recalling other memorable events that occurred when the two aunts paid that last visit in 2008.

They had exchanged abuse over the phone while trying to fix a date for their arrival, and it was finally his mother, Denise, who had bravely intervened. She rang them both, and personally fixed the timetable for their visit. As soon as they had each begrudgingly accepted the proposal individually, and without consulting one another, Jack quickly prepared a fishing holiday for himself and two old friends on the Isle of Wight. He had told his son sternly to stay at home because it would be important for somebody to protect his mother if total, physical war broke out.

"Anyway," he had said, with a grin and patting him affectionately on the head, "it will give you the opportunity to brush up on your French and I am sure you will learn a lot of new words."

Denise had protested lamely and Jack had stuck out his tongue.

To avoid the first pitched battle, Denise had organised the allocation of bedrooms. Aunt Charlotte would have the spare bedroom and Aunt Gisele would have the fold-out bed in Jack's study.

"I'm the eldest, I should get the real bedroom," Aunt Gisele had protested.

Before Aunt Charlotte had time to protest, Daniel's mother had faced the two of them with her hands on her hips.

"If you are not in your allocated rooms within the next ten minutes, mouths closed, unpacking your bags, I will drive you back to the ferry", she had announced firmly.

Daniel started making notes because he knew that his father would be eager for a report as soon as he got home. He called them 'les *vieilles folles'* (the crazy old women), but never to their face.

When they came back from their rooms, the second drama occurred. Unknowingly, they had bought the same blue and white skirt. My poor mother could not help laughing. They were furious, glaring first at my mother, then at one another.

Gisele had finally shrugged her shoulders.

"My skirt is an original from a reputed *couturier,* Charlotte's is just a vile copy," she had announced haughtily.

Before Gisele could prepare her riposte, Denise had fired a lovely reply.

"I do a lot of shopping on the Internet," she had explained sweetly. I recognise that skirt; I saw it on the M & S Mode site on sale for 39 Euros."

There was a moment of silence, and then each aunt decided to sulk. Denise had winked at her son, but they were not silent for long. They had moved into that very special debate the family knew so well, during which each contestant tried to prove that she was poorer, unhappier and sicker than the other. It all came out over afternoon tea. They had seated ourselves around the table in the conservatory, surrounded by lovely plants, sipping Earl Grey and munching ginger biscuits, when the debate had begun.

"I only sleep about four hours a night," Charlotte had announced with a heavy sigh.

I don't sleep at all," poor Gisele had replied. "That's why I have to take Deprimac 50 for stress."

Charlotte had uttered a bitter laugh as she tackled her fifth biscuit.

"Lucky you!" she had exclaimed. "I've been on Deprimac 100 for years!"

They had actually agreed on one point. If Charlotte's husband had retired on a very small pension, and Gisele's husband had been on the dole for half of his life, they did acknowledge that both husbands were worthless.

"That probably explains why neither of you had children," Denise had commented with a loving smile.

Daniel had grinned too, because he remembered his father saying one day that God had should have given them one daughter each so that the constant bickering could be upgraded with the next generation: via Facebook, for example.

Daniel remembered that year so well. One evening, over dinner, he and his mother learned that Gisele's dishwasher had broken down, while Charlotte had never been able to afford a dishwasher. Charlotte had not gone to Gisele's daughter's wedding, while Gisele had not attended Charlotte's daughter's communion. Charlotte's husband had sold his very old car, a Renault 12, to make both ends meet while Gisele's husband had never owned a car because they were too poor.

At that stage, Denise had become very angry and had stormed out of the room to come back a few minutes later to toss on the table a collection of photos she had received from her sister, who lived in Paris, and who had visited the two aunts a few months before. In them, they saw Charlotte and her husband posing next to their new Saab, while Gisele and her husband were proudly polishing a very smart Peugeot 407. Not only did they both own nice cars, Denise had pointed out, very loudly, but they were both smiling in the photos, something she had never had the privilege of witnessing.

There was a moment of horrified silence, before the two aunts had resumed their meal in stony silence.

The year 2008 had seen the worst visit by far. They fought over the remote control for the TV, though neither of them understood a word of English. There was a bidding session where each tried to have higher blood pressure than her sister until Denise had to remind them that with the latest figures announced they were both clinically dead. They had even fought over who hated the other the more intensely. Daniel had the impression that in this case Gisele won, but preferred not to express an opinion.

His mother had told him that they were both excellent cooks, but he never saw an example of their skills. That year, they watched Denise cook each meal, standing in the kitchen, arms crossed across their ample bosoms, each sister reminding the other that her cooking skills were appalling. Before the meal each sister would produce a pill box and count in a loud voice the number of pills she had to take before the meal. Gisele had twelve and Charlotte fourteen, which had allowed the latter to boast proudly that she was sicker than her sister, while Gisele claimed it was only because her doctor was an imbecile.

Finally, after ten days of bickering Denise had interrupted a new battle by announcing loudly that if they did not shut up she would throw them out. An hour later, Charlotte had left in a taxi, heading back to France. Gisele had screamed 'good riddance', shaking her fist at the departing vehicle, and then left ten minutes later. Jack had come home the next day and that evening Daniel heard the laughter, the giggles and the familiar creaking of the four-poster bed. There was no visit in 2009 because the Inghams went to Paris on holiday.

Daniel was still laughing to himself on the bench when his father put his arm around his shoulder and brought him back to reality.

"Come on, son, it's time to go home. You must be tired."

He slept most of the way home in the back seat of their car, and when they opened the front door it was just after one o'clock in the morning. The red light on the telephone answering machine was blinking and Denise listened to the message in French.

"It's from Albert," she said, pronouncing the name the French way 'Albear'. "He asks me to call back whatever the time."

"Who is Albert?" Daniel asked.

"Charlotte's husband," his father explained, and then turning to his wife," Let's wait till tomorrow, we're all tired."

Denise shook her head and her face was pale.

"He insisted," she said, lips trembling. "I have a prenominition."

She spoke for a few minutes, in a low voice and then put down the phone.

"We have to go back tomorrow," she said softly.

"For God's sake, why? Jack asked angrily.

She was crying and Daniel ran towards her to hug her, arms around her waist.

"Charlotte died an hour ago in hospital," she explained softly. "There was an accident, she missed a corner on the coastal road driving home and drove her car into the sea."

There was a moment of silence.

"She was alone?" Jack asked.

Denise nodded

"Yes. Albert had said it was late and had decided to spend the night with old friends but she insisted on leaving."

There was another long silence.

"Do you think that she . . . . ?" Jack left the question open.

Denise mother shrugged.

"Who knows? I often thought that behind all that bickering was a strong bonding and affection."

"You're right," Jack decided. "We must go back. I'll call the office tomorrow morning to warn them."

As Daniel snuggled up in his bed, trying to find sleep, he tried to imagine Aunt Charlotte arriving at the Pearly Gates where Aunt Gisele, arms crossed over her bosom, would be waiting for her.

What do you want?" Gisele would have shouted. "We don't want you here!"

"It's not my fault," Charlotte would have protested. "It was an accident!"

"You were never a good driver!" Gisele would have shouted back, before taking her sister in her arms, to whisper in her ear. "You were too lonely without me that was the problem."

Daniel fell asleep with tears on his cheeks. Perhaps in heaven they had finished bickering.

PETER GRAHAM AND THE FACE IN THE BUCKET

After the first annual school concert, the other kids at Blaxford primary school knew Peter Graham was a freak. The other women tossed scornful looks at his mother, with her loud French accent, her short skirts and her heavy make-up.

"Peter Graham's mother looks like a whore!", he heard William Crompton's mother mutter angrily.

They would have been surprised to know that she taught domestic sciences in a Catholic school in Ashmeadow.

"What about the father?" Mrs Williams asked loudly. "Can't see him here!"".

Unfortunately, Peter's father had left his mother some ten years ago, when the boy was still a baby and the only souvenir he had was a photo of him walking out of the building where he worked in Little Collins Street. That day, as usual, his father wore his pin-striped suit, his black felt homburg hat and his umbrella. He was a financial advisor with the Sabatini group, but in his dreams he was still working in the City of London where his career began.

Peter's French grandmother was pleased to hear that he had gone.

"He was an imbecile," she told her daughter on the phone from Lyon where she ran a milliner's shop. "I know that he ran away to settle in Fiji with an air hostess, but you should tell people he was killed on safari in Kenya, it's much more *chic*. As I have always said, never judge a man by the cut of his coat. Come back to France and bring that little idiot Peter with you!"

Peter's mother was a determined woman, like her own mother, and she refused. So there stood poor Peter, a schoolboy without a father and with a mother who dressed like a sixties starlet and who spoke with an almost unintelligible accent. He also had curly hair, he wore glasses, he was a little overweight (mother's cooking!) and he was acutely shy and thus the favourite punching bag in the school yard. Punches, kicks and taunts were stable ingredients in his daily diet, a therapy against differentness that the other kids in Blaxford primary school thought might be effective. He was tripped, punched and kicked during basketball matches, staunchly putting up with the pain and the humiliation. His mother wanted to go and pick a fight with the school principal, but he talked her out of it. Finally, one humiliating day, insulted, scorned, bruised, scathed, with two broken teeth and a heavily fractured self-esteem, he lost his cool and punched William Crompton on the nose, sending bright red blood pouring down his shirt.

Susie Williams, the most beautiful girl in the class, clasped her hands together and beamed at him.

"You are a hero, Peter Graham," she whispered, and he knew she was right.

He got home that evening, glasses held together with insulating tape but with a very high opinion of himself, for the first time in his life. From that day on, he was known as the school bully, and taunts were only thrown at him from a very safe distance. His mother was delighted, but he knew that he was still that timid boy who flinched when somebody shouted near him and who blushed a deep shade of purple when a girl spoke to him. Sandra Bingham tried to kiss him once behind the Blaxford municipal library and he nearly died; of shame or of fear, he was not quite sure.

"You have to get out and meet people," his mother decided.

From that year on, and despite his protestations, she would sent him to holiday camp where he would live with total strangers and eat holiday food with other kids whose families could not afford a real holiday. As he grew up, he began to suspect that his absence allowed his mother to enjoy a little freedom.

Mrs Bates, a neighbour and a cruel gossip, confirmed his suspicions.

"I saw that French tart next door, when I was quite accidentally looking through her kitchen window, yesterday morning," she told the butcher while Peter was buying sausages. "There was a bald man with a thick moustache draped in one of her ridiculous dressing gowns eating crumpets and marmalade."

The butcher was trying desperately to draw the spiteful woman's attention to the fact that the 'French tart's' son was standing next to her, but she pursued her tirade with determination.

"He was sitting on Peter's chair at the kitchen table, very early in the morning,"she announced. "What does that tell you?"

Peter made the mistake of telling his mother what the neighbour had said and ten minutes later she rang the Bates doorbell. When Mrs Bates opened the door, she received a free and frank consultation.

"You're a frigid old bitch," his mother announced, delving into the psychology lessons she had picked up from Readers Digest. "You husband probably ran away to avoid your dirty mouth, and you are jealous because I have active and healthy hormones."

From that day on, Terry Bates would not speak to him in class or in the playground.

Even when he moved up to Blaxford Grammar, the summer holiday remained the great event in his life. He liked the novelty of meeting strangers, other lost souls like himself, sometimes from far-away planets like Adelaide, Brisbane or Ireland. It was far, far better than staying at home to listen tohis mother and her gentlemen friends drinking and laughing and keeping him awake at night.

It was the summer of 1992. Mother had been invited by a new friend to travel to the Barossa Valley in his posh Volvo where they would spend a month together. She probably thought she was in love.

"I have a wonderful holiday for you this year, Peter," she announced, eyes sparkling with excitement. "This time, it will be different. You are going to spend a whole month with the Hamilton family on their farm about thirty kilometres from Hobart, in beautiful Tasmania. You will be giving French lessons to their daughter."

Peter had just turned sixteen. He had pimples and the sheer sight of a girl in a miniskirt terrified him. To add to his misery, it was his first flight and the turbulence when they landed in Hobart scared him to death. The Hamilton family had an apple orchard and produced cider, but they also grew potatoes and carrots and raised goats, pigs, chicken and ducks. The father, Ben, who was a self-declared anarchist, had his own slaughter house where he converted the chicken and ducks into pâté and the pigs into a sausage called the Hamilton Hunger, totally unknown outside of Tasmania. His wife, Alice, cooked, sowed, made jams and milked the goats to make cheese and yoghurt. There was a grandmother whom he never saw, who lived in a room in the attic, often playing the accordion.

He was sitting on a bench in the yard one morning when he heard her play 'Under the Bridges of Paris' and wondered where she had learned the song. He would have liked to meet her but Alice told him she was crazy and could be quite dangerous, so he should keep away. He could not believe that a little old lady who played "Red Sails in the Sunset' every evening with such talent could be wicked.

Ben was quite frightening. When he was not strangling chickens and ducks or cutting the throats of some poor little piglets, he would wander around the wood with an axe on his shoulder, muttering to himself and occasionally taking wild swipes at nearby trees.

Alice seemed to spend most of her day shouting abuse at all the others, complaining about the dreadful life she led, and when she made an omelette she beat the eggs with such vigour that Peter had the impression that they were being punished for all the dreadful things inflicted on her by the other members of the family. Her only joy was her elder son.

Ben and Alice had three children, two boys called Charlie and Paul, both in their late teens, and a daughter called Christine who was fourteen and with whom he was to undertake French conversation lessons. The farm was quite large and included a pond, a small creek and a large barn full of machinery, tools, straw and many strange objects he could not identify. He had the feeling that a few days could have been well spent cleaning up a lot of useless rubbish, but the kids did not seem to suffer from super-activity.

Christine suggested that they undertook the French lessons in the barn where they could make themselves a cosy little nook between bales of straw. She thought that she would learn much faster and with less embarrassment if she was far from her mother's ears and eyes. Peter claimed to suffer from hay fever and claustrophobia. He preferred the large kitchen where there was fresh air, sunshine, plenty of passing traffic, and where he could keep a large wooden table between himself and a young lady who, he quickly discovered, was determined to explore the physical attributes of the average young male. He was too terrified to be a prominent participant in her research.

Charlie, the elder son, was obviously the seducer of the village, to judge by the number of girls who seemed to fight for his favours, usually delivered in the back of an old camper-van standing on blocks next to the pond. When delights were under way, his mother stopped screaming abuse and listened to the activity from her kitchen window, a smile of absolute delight on her face. When the favoured young lady left, always on foot, mother would make a note in a little diary.

"Was that Mary Foster?" she would call out loudly, for example.

And her son would emerge from the van, a wicked smile on his face. Inevitably, Alice would be wrong and he would tell her that it was in fact Margaret Dunk or Frances Goddard.

Paul, the second son, was about sixteen and spent most of the summer holidays in a hammock slung between two apple trees where he would read old copies of Playboy. He only spoke to Peter once and that was to declare that if he dishonoured his sister he would cut his throat with one of his father's slaughtering knives. Peter remembered that his mother always told him to be wary of the quiet, silent types, they were the most dangerous.

Three days after his arrival, the evening concert stopped. Grandmother and the accordion had disappeared and Alice spent the following weekend cleaning out the top floor. The stench from Ben's cooking pot, perched on large bundle of firewood, was appalling.

"The pigs are going to have a wonderful feast," he told Peter with a wicked wink.

"And we will be able to rent out the attic," Alice added, flicking imaginary dust out of the air.

Because he did not want to die young, and, above all, so far away from his mother and his schoolmates, he asked no questions. That night he slept badly, his trembling causing the iron-frame bed to squeak continually. Nothing, nothing could make him climb up to the attic!

The next morning he walked, pale-faced, into the kitchen where Alice ignored him. That morning, and for the following days, he continued to avoid intimate French lessons with Christine. She wore the shortest skirts he have ever seen and covered her lips with a thick coating of fluorescent lipstick. He had the impression that she had stuffed a pair of rugby socks in her T-shirt to make herself more attractive, and she walked wobbling her hips to draw his attention.

He came to the conclusion that the activities of her elder brother excited her curiosity, and that she had decided that her sexual education could only come to a fruitful outcome with the help of the only male victim on hand. She was not interested in foreign languages but foreign affairs. Occasionally her antics would draw the attention of her mother and she would be rewarded with a slap in the face that would have knocked the head off a cat.

His refuge was the magnificent wood next to the property, a place where he could escape Christine and live a world of imaginary adventures. He was Robert Hall, famous policeman, pursuing the terrible Ned Kelly, protecting innocent travellers and fair maidens on the dangerous highway. He was intrepid, until he heard the voice of Christine in the distance, calling him in wooing tones.

"Peter, Peter my darling, where are you!" She would call in what she thought was a syrupy voice.

He applied an old adage, learnt from his mother, ensuring his safety in flight!

He had to admit that Alice, the mother was a marvellous cook. Each meal was a like a visit to a gastronomic paradise. She loved to watch the 'poor skinny, under-nourished boy' eat with such enthusiasm, and abused her poor husband for not showing as much pleasure with her fine cooking. He nearly choked once during a meal when Christine's hand came exploring under the table and Charlie, sitting opposite him, laughed at his embarrassment. Nobody else in the family seemed to notice the incident.

Even when he was deep in the woods, he could hear Alice, the mother, shouting or screaming. He was fast developing a new vocabulary of abusive or insulting words. She seemed to be in a permanent state of anger with her husband, her stove, her washing machine, the postman and the vacuum cleaner. Her only kind words were for her goats or for her elder son. His amorous victories delighted her and Peter suspected it was less for the expression of his male domination as for the humiliation each conquest might inflict on a neighbouring family.

Peter's mother had once told him that many mothers delight in the conquests of their sons and fiercely protect the innocence of their daughters. Unfortunately, Alice was not paying enough attention to her daughter, he told himself, as he escaped, again, a grappling attack while helping to load the dishwasher.

He became quite accustomed to Alice's screaming abuse. It accompanied his breakfast, overshadowed his dinner and sent him into a fitful sleep at night. When he went into the village with her husband to help him with the shopping, the sudden silence was almost frightening. Ben explained to him one day that his wife no longer went into the village because she had abused so many shopkeepers that she was not welcome. He told Peter that one day Colette, the hairdresser, had even closed her shop and locked the door when she saw Alice coming down the street.

Usually the shopping expedition ended with a short stop in the pub, where Ben seemed to have many sympathetic friends.

"Come on, Ben, another one for the road," Ted would shout.

"And how's that lovely wife of yours?" Stan would enquire with a wink and a nudge.

Once they reached home, Alice would smell the beer on his breath.

"You've been drinking again!" she would scream. "Wasting our good money on filthy booze!"

The screams of abuse would increase in volume and pitch until Ben shrugged his shoulders and walked away.

It was a Thursday. Ben had slit the throat of a pig and was gathering blood in a bucket to eventually make black pudding. As the animal died, Peter realised that he was singing. He had never heard Ben sing. It was that 'People will say we're in Love' song written by Rodgers and Hammerstein for Oklahoma, one of Peter's mother's old-time favourites. Nobody could accuse Ben and Alice of being in love, he thought to himself, but he was surprised to note that the farmer had a beautiful voice.

Peter did not enjoy bloodshed, so he went for a walk around the garden and came back when Ben had finished. There was something oddly quiet about the house today, although there seemed to be some excitement in the camper-van, judging by the giggles.

Later, Peter saw a tall red-head emerge from the vehicle of love, exchanging passionate kisses with a gloating Charlie. Another one bites the dust, he told himself. He returned to the little slaughter house to see that Ben was now stuffing large lumps of meat into the mincer.

"We will soon have fresh sausage meat", he announced gaily, surrounded by his buckets. "I have promised a load to the butcher if you would like to come with me this evening?"

This evening? What would Alice think of that, he wondered?

He nodded and stood beside him, watching him work. Quite by accident, he looked down into one of the buckets. Alice's face was staring back at him.

No wonder it was so quiet today, he told himself. And where was grandmother? Had she been the ingredient of that delicious Irish stew?

He would have some extraordinary things to tell his mother if he ever got home.

THE LIFE OF A STAR

In the sixties, most of the residents of Blaxford had heard of the singer and songwriter who called himself Austin Freeway. There had even been an attempt to create the Ozzie Freeway Fan Club, but membership never got much above a hundred people and by the early seventies the club had disappeared. In 1964, the local radio station had run a short programme with an interview of Austin Freeway and samples of his music. They broadcast his three most popular songs, 'An 'orse Called Reginald', 'On the Road to Wangaratta' and 'Me Wife's Up the Duff".

Unfortunately, he never could adapt his voice to the Texan accent so important in Country Music and the closest he got to the Tamworth Country Music Festival was running a Candy Floss stand at a fair in Quirindi. His fans reckoned that he had been Humphrey Bear for a few weeks in 1968, but it was only a rumour.

His longer term success was as an imitator. He started with some fairly ordinary take-offs of Frankie Lane and Buddy Holly but his great success came the night he decided to sing Nat King Cole's 'Pretend' at the Albury Soldiers, Sailors and Airmen Club. He was gratified with four encores and six cartons of Victoria Bitter and after he had packed himself and his gains into his old Nissan Bluebird, he drove south, believing that fame was just around the next bend on the Hume Highway.

When he got back to Blaxford, he boasted so much in the local pub of his sudden popularity that Fred Parton, nicknamed 'Dolly', offered to become his agent. Austin thought that this was a sure sign of success as 'Dolly' already managed many famous regional artists such as Rubber Girl, Doreen and the Doorknobs, Mabula the Magician and 'Spider' Webb and his Golden Flute.

In every man's career there is a peak. In Austin's case, the peak lasted just over a year. He was an attraction in regional theatres in Sutton Vale and Ashmeadow, at the Annual Rotary Ball in Midvale, provided aged care sing-song afternoons in Newbridge and performed at country race meetings in Blaxford, but after a while people were saturated with 'Pretend' and 'Answer Me, My Love'. Unlike Paul McCartney or Sandy Shaw, Austin was not producing a new number every month. He told his fans that he liked tradition; His critics reckoned that he was just bone lazy.

Within two years the Austin Freeway phenomenon was over. F.J.Holden was a national star, and a pseudo Frenchman called Maurice Minor was making a killing in the West with his imitations of Maurice Chevalier. Austin was offered the job of ticket collector at the Blaxford railway station, and he entertained travellers commuting from Melbourne after a hard day's work by singing 'Answer me, my love' as they handed in their tickets. The station master was quite chuffed by the idea, and Win TV offered a short video of the singing ticket collector on regional news. It was fun, it was flattering, but it did not create any new career opportunities.

When good fortune comes to people in East Malvern, Balwyn, Toorak or Brighton it arrives delicately, on tip-toes, humming like an Audi Quattro on cruise control and smelling of '*L'Air du Temps*' de Nina Ricci. When it deserts somebody in regional Victoria, it wears hob-nailed boots, smells of cow dung and is accompanied by a bottle of Bulgarian Vodka. Austin Freeway sank slowly into ethanol oblivion until success struck, suddenly and unexpectedly.

It came in the form of a letter, typed on one of those antique machines called typewriters. It was signed by the Consul General of Krakovia, a democratic republic of Eastern Europe which, like all countries called 'democratic republics', was a dictatorship. It invited Austin to come to Pizov, the capital, and once there to the Presidential palace, to offer a recital of the best songs ever interpreted by Nat King Cole.

Austin showed the letter to his agent Fred, that same night in the Blaxford Arms, and 'Dolly' undertook a little research on the Internet. He reported to Austin and his fans the next evening, during happy hour.

"You gotta be joking," he announced. "This Krakovia is a tiny country, a bit bigger than Phillip Island at low tide. It got its independence when the Soviet Union broke up, probably because it has no resources that could interest the Russian Mafia."

"I don't care," Austin replied stubbornly. "I'm going anyway. It's the beginning of my international career."

There were a few sniggers in the public bar.

"There's a blog that says it hasn't got an Embassy in Canberra because it wanted to build a traditional Krakovian building."

"What's the problem?" Steve, a long-time fan asked. "I thought that's what all countries did."

Fred laughed.

"A traditional Krakovian building has walls of dried camel dung and a corrugated tin roof," he explained.

"So there's no ambassador?" Austin asked.

"Not really," Fred replied. "If you look up 'diplomatic representation' on the internet you'll find an honorary consul called Red Grogov who lives in Carrington Inlet."

"I've heard of him," said Barry Pescia. "He's one of the best surfers on the coast."

Austin met the Consul General in his office, an old VW camper van parked near the beach. He had stopped in a bottle shop on the way, having been warned that the fee for a tourist visa was a six pack of Corona. He should have taken two packs.

"It's the new President who wants to see you," Red explained, wiping the froth from his Stalin-styled moustache with the back of his hand. "He lived for a few years in Victoria, he studied woodwork in a TAFE for about five years, and he was a fan of yours."

"I'm not surprised," Austin said modestly.

"Pity about your name, though," Red Grogov commented. "I thought your name was Austin Freeway, but on your passport it says your Peter Flanagan, born in Maverton Plains".

Austin shrugged his shoulders.

"Freeway's my professional name. Will that be a problem?"

The honorary consul took another swig from the bottle.

"Nah, I'll just stick an entry visa in your passport, no worries."

Austin gazed proudly at the new stamp in his new passport. The national emblem of Krakovia was a bald cockerel perched on an empty bottle of vodka.

Austin's had never travelled overseas before and he was a little nervous. To make things worse, the trip was complicated, because to reach Krakovia, he had to transit through six different countries. He travelled on some exotic aircraft, notably a Lockheed Electra, a DC4, a Caravelle, a Focker Friendship, a Tupolev 144 and a Yak 40. His Yak 40 landed at the Aleksei Buggerov International Airport at dawn, and while waiting to pass through customs he was able to read a pamphlet in English thrust into his hand by a ground hostess with gold-capped teeth. It explained that the airport was named after a local citizen who had bravely participated in two Salyut space flights.

The two representatives of Customs, Immigration, Quarantine and Forceful Expulsions hated his passport.

"You are not Austin Freeway, you are not Nat King Cole, you are Peter Flanagan!" a customs officer shouted at him. "You are a spy and you will be shot!"

Luckily, a representative of the Palace was there to greet him and he immediately issued a new certificate of citizenship, drawn up on the back of a grubby envelope, classifying him as a pardoned foreign spy called Nakin Cole. As the customs officer was dragged away towards the salt mines, Austin was whisked away and a chauffeur drove him to the presidential palace in a Zil 114 without shock absorbers. The representative of the Palace, a charming red-head called Olga, held his trembling hand all the way.

"You will be very happy here," she whispered, running an inquisitive tongue around his ear. "In my country, everyone is happy. It is a presidential order."

On arrival, Austin was amazed to be greeted by an old friend as he stepped out of the car.

"Pisspot!" he cried out in delight, hugging the old friend in his arms. He had immediately recognised a foreigner who had spent a few years in his home town, a man who had been nicknamed Pisspot a few years ago by some of the regulars in the local pub. True to style, Pisspot was wearing an Essendon T-shirt, boxer shorts and thongs.

"Careful," Pisspot whispered in his ear as they hugged a second time. "Here you have to call me 'President'".

Austin was delighted to learn that Pisspot had organised a barbecue in the palatial gardens rather than a formal banquet in his honour, Camel meat sausages would be burnt in his honour and washed down with Bordeaux wine imported from Ukraine. That night, President Pisspot assured him that a young virgin, one of his forty chamber maids, would accompany him to his bedroom where, if he so chose, she would attend to his needs.

"I'm not really into virgins," Austin pleaded." Jet lag, probably."

Pisspot laughed, slapped him on the shoulder.

"Do not be modest, my friend," he shouted." The lady I have chosen for you had already received a Medal of Valour from a visiting Italian Minister of Defence and a Legion of Honour from a French President.

That's great", Austin pleaded. "But a good Aussie boy was very different to a visiting European politician and I'd rather carry on with a slab or two of a local beer, coleslaw, snags and mateship, with no sheilas on the horizon."

President Pisspot looked disappointed, and Austin realised that he was on dangerous ground.

"In any case," he added, blushing, "if there is one virgin in the Presidential palace tonight, it's probably me."

The President graciously accepted the change of programme with a smile. But the party was not yet over. After the barbecue, the several hundred guests gathered in the ballroom where Austin, or Nakin Cole as he was now called, began his world famous repertoire: *Answer me, my love, Pretend, Mona Lisa, Rambling Rose, Too Young* were rolled out in his usual style, each song followed by enthusiastic applause.

In the middle of his greatest success, something extraordinary happened to Austin-Nakin that evening. He cast his eyes on the President's sister, Olga Nathalie, a blushing young thirty-year old, and fell in love. She had watched his performance, eyes humid with emotion, lips trembling with passion, while deep gasps of delight lifted a pair of 85 C's full of promise.

A few months later, Dolly and the fans in the public bar of the Blaxford Arms received an amazing letter. Austin-Nakin had been appointed Under-Secretary for Popular Music and Hydroponic Agriculture, although, for language reasons, his wife, Olga Nathalie, delivered all his political speeches. A statue had been raised in his honour at the entrance of the international airport car park, showing Austin-Nakin smashing a pile of US dollars with a sledgehammer. The motto underneath declared 'Bugger Capitalism!'

Two years later, Sky News announced that a revolution had overturned the government, the President had fled to Monaco and that Krakovia was now a kingdom. Clients at the Blaxford Arms saw his majesty on SBS news one night and everyone in the pub swore that it was their old mate Austin Freeway. He called himself King Cole, but they knew it was Austin wearing a red wig.

The fact that the new national anthem sounds almost exactly like *Rambling Rose* confirmed their suspicions.

CATCHING UP SWITH OLD FRIENDS

"Life is like crossing a long, dark lake," Curly said whimsically as he made a second attempt to stroke Brenda's large breast. "For some, it will be calm and placid, for others rough and choppy, for others again, full of dangerous whirlpools."

Sunsets made Curly romantic.

For the second time, his hand was pushed away very gently. They were sitting on a grassy knoll overlooking Lake Durrington, watching the sun drop towards the water. The lights of Sutton Vale glimmered behind them in the twilight. The curvaceous sales assistant from Murdoch's News World was not a snob, and she enjoyed sharing a beer now and again by the lake with the town's bad boy, on the way home from work. She had decided that the social outcast was not only a clever juggler and an excellent accordionist but a philosopher who was happy to share little snippets of general knowledge which she stored in her personal data bank, using them when appropriate during the pub quiz on Friday nights.

"You know that some people wanted to change the lake's name," Brenda said, watching a fleet of ducks swim past.

Curly shook his head.

"No, never heard that."

"Yeah, they wanted to call it Lake Anderson, after Raymond Anderson, a bloke who disappeared with his canoe about ten years ago."

Curly smiled.

"Sounds like a silly idea to me. Stick to traditions, I say."

Brenda nodded.

"Yeah, that's what the council said. But why is it called Lake Durrington?"

"It's named after John Durrington, a bloke who found silver in the hills around here about two hundred years ago," Curly explained. "You can store that away, it will probably come up in the Friday night quiz one of these days."

Brenda laughed and looked at her watch.

"I'll remember that. Were you here when Anderson disappeared?"

Curly nodded.

"I'd just arrived. It was almost exactly ten years ago. He was well known here, the general manager of a chain of bottle shops belonging to the Sabatini group. It seems that he jumped into his canoe for a paddle round the lake, as he did most Saturdays. His wife rang the police Saturday evening to say he hadn't come home. It wasn't until Monday, no, wait Tuesday, that somebody found the canoe and the police searched for another week for the body but found nothing."

"Funny that the body's never turned up," Brenda commented. "Not like that poor Mrs Hutchinson who suddenly came to the surface last year!"

Curly laughed.

"Sergeant Wise was pleased to grab the Colonel," he commented. "Pompous old bastard, he was. Prison will bring him down to Earth."

Brenda nodded. "A real champion, our Trevor."

Curly changed the subject.

"They reckon there's a giant eel living in a hidden cave under the lake. It probably gobbled him up."

Brenda shivered.

"Was Trevor Wise a cop here already when it happened?

Curly nodded.

"Yeah. He's a pig-headed bloke, our Trevor. He wouldn't give up looking for a solution to a crime, but the authorities called off the enquiry after four years. Trevor used to say that the insurance policy was the key."

Brenda raised a plucked eyebrow and passed back the nearly empty bottle.

"What insurance?" she asked.

"The life insurance, Curly explained. "Ray was insured against accidental death with Globe Providence Insurance. His wife, Julia, picked up four million dollars and she spent a few hundred thousand on that house she calls *Blue Vista*."

"Cool!" Brenda exclaimed, and for a moment, they stared silently across the lake at the magnificent home sitting alone on a promontory.

"The locals say that she's always on her terrace looking out over the lake with those big binoculars of hers," Brenda said. "Maybe she's still hoping to see him come home."

Curly laughed.

"You mean she's hoping to see him climb out of the lake with holes in the place of his eyes and his body covered in weeds?"

Brenda shuddered again, and sighed.

"You can laugh. I still think she spends her life waiting for her Raymond."

Curly laughed again.

"You read too many of those girly magazines in your shop," he suggested. "She's probably got a lover hidden up there."

Brenda smiled, standing up and brushing grass from her skirt.

"It's late, I'd better get home. Where are you sleeping tonight?"

Curly shrugged his shoulders.

"I always find a place. And no, I don't want hospitality, I like being alone."

Brenda hopped on her bike and began the short ride around the lake shore to her home. Curly walked slowly back up the small Sutton Vale shopping mall, turning on to Robinson Street to sit down on a stone seat opposite the Chinese Restaurant. As the sun slipped behind McCaffrey Hill, a dark car slid to a halt in front of the fountain, a door opened a shadowy figure slipped into the car. The door closed, and the vehicle sped away.

Every first Saturday in April, Sutton Vale celebrated the birthday of the town's founder, a preacher called John Sutton, with a special community party. There was a brass band, marching girls, and Bruce Conduit, a retired dentist, would burn sausages on a barbecue for the Rotary Club while the Mayor would make one of his long-winded speeches to get the party under way. All the shops would offer birthday bargains and promotions.

One of the attractions of the town festival was Curly the tramp. Although neither council nor chamber of commerce employed him, Curly would spend all day in the mall dressed up as a clown, juggling balls, distributing balloons or playing old songs on his accordion. At the end of the day, several shopkeepers would offer him little gifts to thank him for his contribution, such as a shirt from Sutton Vale Menswear, an apple pie from the Lightfoot bakery, or a bottle of wine from Jack White, manager of the local Sabatini Discount Liquor.

That year, it was around three in the afternoon and the crowd was slowly dwindling. An exhausted Curly had stopped pumping his accordion and was sitting under a tree by the lake, enjoying a bottle of beer.

Suddenly, John Tinney, the jeweller, came running out of his shop, shouting that he had been robbed. It was rumoured that many of his customers believed that if robbery there ever was in Sutton Vale, John was probably the author, but this time it was apparently a real crime. The safety and integrity of the Sutton Vale community was at stake.

Ten minutes later, the police station's new Renault Megane roared up the mall. It was the only vehicle in town allowed there during daylight, and the young driver, Constable McHugh, was enjoying every minute. He pulled the vehicle to a halt with a spin of the steering wheel and a grab on the hand brake, leaving beautiful black burnt rubber marks on the pink paving. Shaken but unhurt, Sergeant Wise, known in the pub as 'Trev', stepped out of the vehicle. He strode towards the jewellers shop where John Tinney stood in the doorway wringing his hands.

"Somebody's taken the Blaxford Banger!" he wept.

The gold nugget known as the Banger had been discovered by Tinney's grandfather, and had been in the Tinney family for three generations. It was the trademark in many ways of the jeweller's business. It sat in a glass cabinet in the middle of the shop for all to admire.

One may say many things about Sergeant Wise, but nobody had ever criticized his efficiency. The cabinet's glass bore some very visible and sticky fingerprints on its surface, which he photographed immediately. The jeweller and his staff were severely questioned by Wise and McHugh and a list of visitors was established. The sergeant then stepped back into the mall, pushed through the throng of admirers and stopped face-to-face with Curly.

"Curly, I'm sorry but because you have been hanging around all day I must take your fingerprints immediately," he explained gently.

The crowd murmured loudly. Curly was a refugee migrant who had been granted permanent residency. Nobody remembered his name, it sounded Serbian, but they knew that he had applied for Australian citizenship, and he was a popular man in the community. Somebody in the crowd called out that he was not the odd one in the town, and offered names of a few other undesirables, including the man from Family First, door-knocking Jehovah Witnesses and a representative selling anti-wrinkle cream. Curly smiled reassuringly at the crowd and held out his hands to prove his willingness to co-operate with the forces of law and order.

Two days later, Trevor Wise received a letter from the jeweller's wife. Barbara Tinney was in Noosa with an ex-trainer from the North Melbourne Football Club and was holding the Banger until her husband agreed to sign the divorce agreement that included a generous monthly allocation to cover her future expenses. She admitted that they were her greasy fingerprints on the glass case; she had just finished a toasted sandwich before knocking off the Banger.

The town laughed when the news came out, but the event had inadvertently given Sergeant Trevor Wise the solution to an old mystery, one that had given him many sleepless nights. He had scrupulously checked Curly's fingerprints with those on record on his files, and had made a discovery that would surprise his critics.

The Megane's tyres crunched the fine gravel of Julia Anderson's magnificent driveway. As Trevor stepped out of the police car, alone for once, to gaze out over the magnificent view over the lake, he wondered how he was going to manage this important conversation. On one hand, he was satisfied that he had brought to a conclusion the only unsolved mystery in Sutton Vale. On the other hand, his decision could create almost a revolution within the community.

Julia Anderson knew that the moment was dramatic. She opened the front door herself. Curly stood next to her, clutching her hand.

"Hello, Curly," Trevor said softly.

Curly smiled.

"We've got a nice pot of Earl Grey and the cook has made some fresh blueberry muffins," he announced.

"That would be nice," Trevor murmured as he stepped across the threshold.

They sat together in the large terrace overlooking the croquet lawn. Trevor placed a Manila folder on the coffee table between them, and his hosts stared at it gravely. Julia poured the tea, Curly passed the muffins and they began to talk.

It was the kind of conversation that could only be enjoyed by good friends, members of a close-knit community living in an idealistic spot overlooking a beautiful lake. There were tears, there were smiles, a little laughter, and even a couple of hugs. Finally, the last muffin consumed, the tea pot emptied for a second time, Trevor stood up, chasing a few crumbs from his trousers with a lace napkin.

He pointed at the file on the coffee table.

"I'll leave that with you, then," he said.

"Thank you,' Julia said picking up the file. "I'll keep it in a safe place. Curly has been granted citizenship and we're getting married next year."

Trevor smiled to himself. How do you marry your own husband, he wondered, or grant Australian citizenship to a man who was already an Australian.

"And Raymond will spend a few more years in the lake," Curly added with a wink.

Trevor Wise shrugged his shoulders.

"It's local folklore. Good for business, attracts a few tourists. Why not? Do you know that the Mayor wants to organise boat trips on the lake at night, next year, with a commentator explaining the Raymond Anderson mystery, and the giant eel in an underwater cave?"

They all laughed.

"What will you do after your retirement?" Curly asked as he accompanied Trevor to his car.

"I'll be moving to Victor Harbour," Trevor admitted. "That's where I was born."

"Six hundred thousand should buy you half the town," Curly suggested, handing him a small envelope. "I'd bank it in Melbourne if I was you."

Trevor put the cheque in his pocket and smiled ruefully.

"Thanks Curly. Whoops, I nearly said Raymond. Pity I will have to leave with one crime unsolved".

"You can't win them all," Curly murmured, patting his old friend on the shoulder.

THE OLD PHILOSOPHERS

From the warm comfort of the vintage Triumph 2500, they watched the girl run along the wind-whipped and deserted beach. She was slim, taut, well proportioned, and the green bikini hugged her greedily. An occasional gust of wind whipped her hair into a flowing copper-coloured mane.

"Bloody marvellous," Stan Cunningham sighed.

"Bloody beautiful," Frank McCabe confirmed, with reserved enthusiasm.

"Where's the mayo?" Bill Bone asked from the back seat rummaging through the picnic basket.

Nobody answered. Stan pulled the tab on the can of light beer and gazed wistfully out over the beach.

"Nowadays, this whole coastline from Carrington to Whittlewood is buggered," Stan declared sadly.

Frank McCabe swallowed the bite he had just taken out of his tuna and beetroot sandwich and nodded in agreement. The girl was now almost out of sight.

"You're right. We're a nation of beach lovers. The pioneers of the Great Outback are the Japanese tourists in air-conditioned Pioneer coaches. They reckon that Ayers Rock sees more people from Kyoto than from Melbourne."

Bill Bone laughed as he watched his two mates still staring at the girl who was disappearing over the horizon.

"You're both old enough to be her grandfather," he chided them. "Look at you, a hundred and fifty years of perving between you. Luckily your pacemakers are fitted with Duracells!"

Frank sighed.

"It's my last perv, so let it be. Apart from beer, it's the only pleasure I get out of life."

Bill didn't agree but he kept quiet.

"There are schools in inner Melbourne that take kids out to the country to see farm animals," Stan said, changing the subject without reason.

"Well, they have to, don't they?" Frank asked. "They don't know that cows have feet and horns, and that they shit in fields. They think that cheese grows in pre-sliced packages."

"Farmers will soon have to buy carbon credits every time their cows fart," Stan announced wisely.

"The world's stuffed, I'm telling you".

Frank waved the remnants of a ham and tomato sandwich towards the horizon.

"My grand-daughter went crazy when her mother explained that eggs came out of a chook's bum. Reckoned she wouldn't eat them any more 'cos they're dirty."

"I bet she washes her hands in antibacterial lotion ten times a day. No wonder the poor kids are allergic to everything. Bit of dirt never did anyone any harm", Frank grumbled.

"They're not even allowed to stroke a dog, have you noticed?" Stan asked. "'Don't touch the puppy darling, you never know where it's been'", he added, imitating the squeaky voice of a Ford-Explorer-driving vegan mother.

His imitation made Stan laugh, but Bill kept quiet. If the truth be known, he was a little tired of hearing his two best mates moan all day long, and he was not too happy with today's outing.

"There are people who come down here on the weekend to sit on the dunes and look out to sea. Do you know why they do that? Because it's bloody beautiful." Bill commented, trying to insert a positive note in the conversation.

"Bullshit! They're dreaming of escape", Stan explained. "They turn their back on their country and gaze towards the lands of their ancestors. They love Melbourne because it reminds them of Milan or Athens or Manchester. They suffer from antipodean cringe."

Bill had to fight hard not to laugh at that expression, but Stan continued his lament.

"They whip out their cheque books when you tell them about orphans in Sri Lanka or the Philippines and they shrug their shoulders when you tell them that are aboriginal kids living in misery," he added.

For once, Bill agreed. As his mates continue to moan about the dreadful world they lived in, he did his favourite trick. He switched off his hearing aid and sank back in his seat to remember the good old days.

Thirty years ago, as complete strangers, all hoping to escape Blaxford, they had met at a land auction and had bought three adjoining blocks in Cockatoo Reach. They had been friends ever since. Curiously, the three old men had lost their wives in quick succession. Bill Bone's missus had died of cancer; Frank McCabe's wife had gone to live in a mobile home in Queensland to be closer to the kids, while Stan Cunningham's old woman had run away to Tasmania with a retired schoolteacher.

Until now, their little town of Cockatoo Reach had resisted the disease that had infested most of the shoreline. To the east, squashed aluminium cans and multi-coloured condoms cover the dunes of Carrington Inlet like so many wild flowers. After dusk, the hollows between the sandbanks echo with the groans and moans of P-plated studs copulating with their grammar school girlfriends.

"The girls are probably high on vodka-raspberry," Frank suggested.

"If the condom breaks, they'll call the baby Sunrise Tequila or Cherry Ripe", Stan added, and Frank laughed.

Bill had just switched his hearing aid back on to overhear the last comments. He thought that each generation had its own way of expressing passion, and that his mates might be just a little jealous of the youngsters. But he kept his thoughts to himself. With a sigh, the three old men packed up their picnic basket, dutifully placed their empty drink cans in a nearby recycling bin and settled down for the quiet drive towards their chosen destiny. Bill slumped down in the back seat, feeling nervous. There was little more than an hour to go. It was supposed to be a unanimous decision, but as was frequently the case, Bill was told by the others what he was going to do. Today he was not going to let the others decide his fate. For the moment, as was his custom, he kept his peace.

Stan pulled the bottle of whisky out of the glove box as Frank steered his old car onto the main road. Nowadays, he rarely drove at over more than sixty kilometres an hour, and today there was no rush. It was their last voyage, and they were on schedule. As they travelled west, they talked wistfully about their youth and their hopes, while the coastal road unrolled itself in front of the windscreen.

Then Stan began his tirade.

Although they knew most of Stan's running commentary by heart, they stilled enjoyed his sarcasm. As they drove past Carrington Inlet, he reminded them that it was here that the jousting knights of the twenty-first century mounted the great waves that sculptured the rugged coastline and rode the curlers that caressed the fine beaches.

Stan's poetic description of the bay and its surfers made them smile.

On the other hand, Frank was quite angry.

"Look at them, look at them," he groaned. "All the glorified homosexuals meet here every evening to celebrate the new Australian culture. Fifty years ago, people would have thrown bottles at them; today, they want them to get married and have children bred in test tubes."

"We are a permissive society," Bill explained quietly. "Today, people live as they choose."

Frank snorted.

"Not me. I'm not permissive; I'm too bloody old fashioned. Do you know that the locals call this whole stretch the Centrelink Coast?" he asked. "It's a sad world."

"But not our world", Stan said sadly. "Not anymore."

Bill said nothing, and his friends almost forgot that he was on the back seat. As they drove further east, Stan and Frank passing the bottle of whisky from one to the other, they reached Cape Headland. Here, the coast forms a succession of bays more popular with the over-forties. Places like Angus Bay still had their fishing community, real people who made a living from the sea. Their homes were of stone or weatherboard and the villages were limited to a corner store/post office, a service station a two-class school and that vibrant monument to Australian civilisation, the country pub. For Stan, Frank and Bill, this was the old-fashioned seaside community they respected. It was an isolated region of the Peninsula, but one they loved.

"The Angus Arms is a real Ozzie country pub," Bill declared. "I love it!"

Stan laughed.

"It used to be," he declared whimsically. "It's still got a public bar with tiled walls, a lounge with fourteen poker machines and toilets that smell of urine. Pity is, today it has a restaurant that offers

'Real Ozzie Tucker'".

"What a joke," Frank moaned. "They put chicken parmy, dim sims, beef wherestheloo with jasmine rice on the menu. No more snags and mash, no more fish and chips. What's Ozzie about that? It's even got tourists with digital cameras!"

"It's very cheap," Bill suggested. "When you're on a pension, it's nice to find a cheap meal."

Frank was right. As they drove past, they saw a couple of coaches in front of the pub, picking up a group of Asian visitors. They had umbrellas, raincoats, jumpers and they were still trying to take photos while the wind whipped their Nike caps off their heads.

"Poor sods," Stan murmured. "Two years savings and a week of hard-earned leave, and what do you get? Angus Bay in autumn. They should have stayed at home."

"I'm sure they're enjoying it all," Bill protested mildly.

When they reached Browne Bluff, Frank drove the Triumph onto the gravel parking area.

"Here we are, guys," he announced softly, switching off the engine.

From where he had parked, the bluff ran down a slight slope for about two hundred yards towards the cliff edge, marked by a frail wooden fence. People would walk down there to take photos of the rock formation in the sea, known as the Three Smugglers. From the car, the three old men could see their own village, Cockatoo Reach, and further away the twinkling lights of Whittlewood on the horizon.

Stan hated Whittlewood. Because it had a beautiful bay with a magnificent backdrop of natural forest, the State government had built a highway that joined the city to the town, so that the snobs from Melbourne could come there for their weekends 'away from it all'. According to Stan, every Friday night, they settled on the beanbags in their four-hundred-square-metre mansions with three plasma TV's, they ordered a Dial-A-Pizza on their mobile phones before texting one another to say how happy they were.

"Horrible place," Frank groaned as he looked at the twinkling lights of the new coastal town. "It's got it all: men with ear-rings, four-wheel-drive Volvos, all-night bars, parking meters, video shops, call girls and financial consultants."

"You forget the all-you-can-eat-for-ten-bucks, the fourteen hairdressers, the buskers, the pharmacy, the dentist, the fortune teller and the new shopping centre", Bill protested. "They've also added a bit of fun and life!"

"I thought people got away for a change", Frank said wistfully, ignoring his back-seat passenger and passing the whisky bottle back to Stan.

"Not this mob," Stan complained. "I bet they'll be asking for an all-night medical centre soon."

They ignored Bill muttering that it might be a good idea.

"They'll soon be in Cockatoo Reach", Frank declared sadly. "When Whittlewood is full, the slimy urban disease will come slipping and sliding down the road, and that will be the end of it all."

"Not our problem anymore", Stan sighed. Frank nodded, but Bill didn't say that he couldn't see a problem with progress.

Frank, Bill and Stan each had a nice timber-clad home in Cockatoo Reach with a veranda all around. Together, they played Five Hundred or Bingo at the Club, and they fished off the beach when the weather was good. Stan thought that the women in the village had fulfilling lives: cooking, washing clothes, doing the housework, making tea for the Pennant players on Saturday afternoons at the Bowling Club. They were even allowed to play carpet bowls on Thursdays. He said that Cockatoo Reach was a community that respected good Australian traditions, but Bill thought privately that not all traditions were necessarily good.

The lawn bowls club was the only social meeting place in Cockatoo Reach, but nowadays it had lost its soul. Four years of drought have reduced the greens to baked earth, and the members played carpet bowls and drank beer indoors while waiting for the rain. In Melbourne, people were still watering their gardens.

"Wait and see", Frank announced. "Soon the people from Whittlewood will turn up with their synthetic greens rolled under their arms.'

"It's not our problem", Stan said, holding the whisky bottle upside down and shaking it to show it was empty.

"Come on Frank, switch her on", Stan said. "You know we're all dying to see what's on the other side".

The engine roared into life and Frank gave one or two jabs on the throttle to warm it up.

"Don't bother, mate", Stan told him. "We're not going far and it's all downhill."

Bill grabbed the door handle and pulled it down slowly while Frank slipped his beautiful old car into gear for the last time, switched on the headlights and let up the clutch. It lurched forward and he quickly moved it through the gears on the dear old column shift. The car accelerated down the slope towards the fence, jumping a few stones, brushing aside a few weeds and shrubs on its way. Nobody on the front seat heard the rear door open and Bill roll to safety, remembering his parachutist training of forty years ago.

Kneeling on the grass, he watched them go. The fence snapped, hardly slowing them at all, and suddenly the old car was airborne. Bill heard Stan let out a great shout.

"Look at the view, Frank! It's bloody marvellous! It's like flying a bloody Spitfire!"

Three years later, Cockatoo Reach had forgotten the two old men. The Trafalgar Fields Lawn Bowls Club had eight synthetic greens and a new clubhouse with sixty poker machines. The bistro served Singapore noodles, soy duck and sushi, although it did offer old-fashioned fish and chips on Fridays. Just for silly old men like Bill.

There are three very exclusive retirement villages there now, each with about sixty town houses, a club with snooker tables, plasma TV and a heated swimming pool, and they form a tidy circle around the new crematorium. The shopping mall throbs with the hum of electric scooters as the old people chased one another from one curiosity shop to another.

There are a couple of benches now on Browne Bluff and a very solid protective fence. Bill Bone sits there some evenings talking to his old friends in his head. God, how he misses them! Bill also talks about them to strangers in the shopping mall, but nobody listens to the ravings of a silly old man. He tells people that he can imagine Frank and Stan, sitting on a celestial cloud, playing Five Hundred and Scrabble and moaning, moaning . . . but nobody listens.

CHARM FADES WITH AGE

Graham Newcombe had difficulties in building up enthusiasm about his son Peter's forthcoming wedding. His closest friend Malcolm had tried to explain his lack of exuberance, several times.

"It's because you stuffed up your own sentimental life," he told him. "You don't want to see him waste his life in the pursuit of what you see as the illusion of marital bliss."

Graham snorted. It was true that two failed marriages and a distasteful break-up with a live-in housemaid on a temporary work visa had made him cynical about all formal types of union. Also, Malcolm seemed to enjoy explaining other people's faults, particularly Graham's. That's what friends are for, according to him.

"You have a total misunderstanding of women," Malcolm insisted. "You also have a knack for always choosing the wrong one. You are also an incurable cynic."

Graham laughed.

"You know bloody well that Peter always rushes headlong into a new adventure, whether it be a job, a car or a girlfriend. I keep telling him to think of the 'Radio Rental' solution: give it a try for six months before deciding if it's the right model."

Malcolm shook his head in despair.

"I told you you were a cynic."

"Bullshit. I'm a realist," Graham corrected. "As a commodity, marriage is useful but not essential. Women seem to enjoy it, and sometimes we have to give in to get what we want. I am a modest man, but have found right back from my youth that women have always found me irresistible."

Malcolm shook his head a second time.

"It must be difficult being perfect and modest at the same time."

Graham ignored the snide comment. He knew that he had always been, and still appeared to be, a good target. Today, at fifty-four years of age, he was handsome, well-dressed, cultivated and looked financially comfortable, in other words exactly the kind of man any ambitious woman between the ages of nineteen and sixty-four would like to trap. Somehow, they imagine him walking through the more exclusive boutiques, smile on his lips, credit cards all fired up, and murmuring simple phrases like 'of course, my darling', or 'no, that's not expensive, why not take two?'

If only they knew the truth. He was not that kind of man at all. Well, not any more.

Graham sighed. Today, and because of another of Peter's impetuous decisions, he was in this small motel in this ugly town called Midvale. His son was an idiot, believing everything he sees and hears. He still thought that his mother, Graham's first wife, was an angel of kindness and generosity. Curiously, he also admired his ex-step-mother, Alice, Graham's second wife. He considered her to be a talented artist, a wonderful hostess and a woman of good taste. The poor idiot had even admired Camille, the housemaid from Quebec.

Graham sighed. The town looked as if it had already gone to bed, at nine o'clock in the evening. Even the street lights were gloomy, and the footpaths were grey and sad. Nothing laughed or danced in this gloomy town where Deal or No Deal was probably the biggest excitement of the day. Standing up from his sagging bed, where had had spent the last ten minutes staring at brown and yellow paintings depicting scenes from the nineteenth century, he walked across to the small en-suite. Gazing at himself in the fly-specked mirror in the dim light, he could see the signs of decrepitude. He was losing his hair, there were those tell-tale flabby spots around his chin, creases around the eyes and his waist line was not where it used to be.

Very soon he would no longer have to fight off passionate admirers.Very soon, he would be perfectly safe, no longer embarrassed when women turned to admire him as he passed by. The realisation comforted him, in some ways. But he also felt a twinge of regret.

He had not seen his son for nearly a year, since Peter had found a job as accountant with Globe Providence Insurance in this God-forsaken dump.When Graham and Alice had divorced, Peter had grown distant, irrationally blaming his father for the breakdown of another marriage. He had not wanted to accept the fact that his father had important social obligations in his job as marketing manager of Maverton Haulage, obligations that took him interstate, wining and dining with agents and customers. If some were of the sweeter sex, it was not his fault, for God's sake! He had no time for the niceties of family life, TV, fish and chip suppers, slippers and hot cocoa. He was an active and popular businessman; he was earning the money they all enjoyed.

Tomorrow, he was attending his son's wedding, and he had never met the bride. Unusually, sudden emotion almost choked him.

He shook his head as if to clear his mind, turned off the bathroom light and stepped back into his bedroom, where only a small bedside lamp was lit.There was now an outside light flashing through the thin curtains. He walked towards the window, pulled back one curtain and saw the bright invitation.The Oasis Cocktail Bar announced to the world that it was a quiet nocturnal haven for the connoisseur of exotic beverages. Being an amateur of all things tasteful or beautiful, he decided to accept the invitation. He snatched up his key from the bedside table and headed for the Oasis to test its claims. He did not expect much, being far from a bustling metropolis, but it might be amusing to see how local fauna tried to entertain themselves.

It was cold and raining slightly as he hurried across the pitch-black, empty street. Dark clouds scudded across the sky but humans were strangely absent. As soon as he pushed open the door he was met by a wave or warm air. He noted immediately that the music was subdued, that Barry White was whispering in the background, and that the club was almost empty. There was a musty smell of ageing carpets and tired wallpaper trying desperately not to fall off the damp walls. There were two couples sipping their drinks and giggling at one table, three men swapping loud jokes at another, and a very attractive girl sitting alone at the bar. He almost wished for a pianist playing 'As Time Goes By' with a Lucky Strike hanging from the corner of his mouth, but finally decided that the sexy baritone would do nicely.

He realised immediately that he was being offered the opportunity to determine whether that good old Graham Newcombe charm was still irresistible. He decided to stick religiously to a proven strategy: feigned indifference. He sat on a stool deliberately several seats away from the target and ordered a Cosmopolitan. It is a popular cocktail, made famous by its promotion in Sex and the City, and its ingredients are vodka, Cointreau and lime and cranberry juice.

The barman nodded happily, and grinned. Even in a small town bar this drink was known, the strategy understood. Graham was not expecting the orange peel garnish and was pleasantly surprised.

The target looked interested. She raised her glass in a silent toast. He played the shy victim. It was going to be very easy, because she slipped off of her stool and walked towards him. She was quite tall, with long black hair and a discreetly curved body. The hugging black dress was obviously expensive, the pendant ear-rings too, and she walked with an elegant sway of her hips that seemed to be quite natural rather than deliberately seductive. She looked as if she was in the mid-twenties, and was definitely not a hooker.

She sat on the stool next to him and extended a hand that he shook gently.

"Tania", she said.

'Graham", he replied.

She looked at his cocktail and raised an inquisitive eyebrow, and he explained its composition. The strategy was working perfectly. He looked at her glass.

"Gin and tonic or vodka and tonic?" he asked.

She hesitated before replying 'yes', which was not really an answer.

At this point Graham remained silent. If he was to succeed he should not look too eager, because this could be interpreted as the attitude of an avid chaser. Anything that was to happen between them must appear to be part of a common acceptance, an exchange of good manners, with no indication of unrestrained lust on the horizon.

"Are you a local resident?" she asked after a few minutes.

"No, I'm from Melbourne. I'm here for a wedding."

She laughed.

"So am I."

He grinned.

"That's the second time that your answer is short on information," he said, teasingly.

She smiled, and held up her glass.

"You're right. First of all this is neither gin and tonic nor vodka and tonic. It's simply sparkling mineral water. As far as the second answer is concerned, I am also from Melbourne and I am here for a wedding."

"We have lots of weddings here," the barman explained, excited by the strategy he knew well. "It's because of the beautiful wedding and conference centres we have in the region."

They both ignored him and he blushed and walked to the other end of the bar, polishing a glass furiously. His opinion had not been sought, and he was not part of the plan. He would admire the imminent victory from a distance.

"You never drink alcohol?" Graham asked. From experience he knew that a glass or two of wine can have a marvellous influence on female relaxation, and that half a bottle of champagne can sometimes encourage a reserved and modest lady of very fine morality to throw her underwear out of a bedroom window.

"A little, in moderation as they say," she explained. "But as I am getting married tomorrow, I want to keep my head clear."

Graham's eyes widened in surprise.

"So you're one of tomorrow's brides?" he asked. "And you are not surrounded by a clucking hen party?"

She laughed.

"The clucking hens do not approve me marrying a man they find boring."

He nodded.

"Preconceived ideas. I hate them," he lied. "I think the marriage I will be attending will face similar problems."

"In any case," she added," I can see no point in going out and making a fool of myself surrounded by drunken giggling girls. I was hoping that tonight a handsome young man might try to charm me for the last time before I tie the knot and 'come off the market' as some of my ruder friends would saw. A girl needs reassuring, even the night before her wedding."

Graham smiled encouragingly.

"Maybe there are not many gallant young men in this small town. But I can assure you, I find you very attractive and quite charming."

She stood up suddenly, placing her empty glass on the bar.

"Are you in the motel across the road?" she asked.

Graham's heart skipped a beat. He had not expected such a fast surrender and emptied his own glass quickly and nodded. The barman polished a second glass feverishly, a grin from ear to ear.

They ran across the street, heads bowed under the rain, her hand on his arm. When they reached the door of his room, he was fumbling for his key when she kissed him awkwardly on the cheek.

"I'll wish you good night," she said. "My room is about six doors away."

He tried not to look disappointed. She took a few steps down the veranda, then stopped and turned.

"By the way", she called out. "We will meet tomorrow. My real name is Catherine, and I am marrying your son. Peter carries your photo in his wallet and you should know that he is very proud of his father."

THE NEW IMMIGRANT

Little Midlow was a small village, eighteen kilometres from Sutton Vale. It straddled a road running between here and there, and the through traffic, travelling from here to there, or in the other direction, would not have represented more than thirty vehicles a day. Potholes in the main street were so old that they have been given names, such as Little Polly which first appeared in front of Granville's Garage during the Vietnam War and had been filled thirteen times since then to no avail.

People passing through Little Midlow rarely stopped because there was nothing to see. The only exciting moments in everyday life were the departure and the arrival of Mr Granville's little red bus, called Reggie, that took people into Blaxford once a day to do their shopping. Even some of the younger residents, those who used neither walking frames nor motorised wheelchairs, used to take the bus now and again just to escape the monotony of a village where nothing ever happened.

The little red bus pulled a little red trailer, called Sally, that carried essential goods: the Blaxford Bugle, fresh milk, canned goods, prescriptions, the mail and other important supplies. All these basic elements of village life were sold or distributed at the Granville Emporium, Milk Bar, Haberdashery & News Agency a forty square feet haven of throbbing commercial life in the village. The only foreign vehicle to stop once a week in Little Midlow was a small brown truck that delivered beer in barrels and other exhilarating beverages in cans or bottles to the Green Dog Inn, the hub of village night-life.

Little Midlow sat on the top of a small hill. The first building a visitor would see coming from the east would be the Emporium, and the last building to be passed heading west was Granville's Garage. At the crest of the hill stood the Green Dog and opposite the Inn was the imposing stone house belonging to the Winkle sisters. Ethel and Mabel were twins, eighty-six years old, reputed to be the most nosey spinsters this State has ever known. All village life was closely monitored by Ethel who managed the binoculars and the six-battery torch mounted on the sill of the second storey window, while Mabel banged out the one-page village gossip page on the old typewriter that sat on the ground floor kitchen table.

A cancerous rot of apathy had gradually consumed the little village. As inhabitants died or left for greener pastures, there were more and more empty houses in the main street. As the years of abandon passed by, paint peeled, gutters leaked, moss grew on pavements and disjointed shutters banged themselves to pieces. Dan Cullen, the village's real estate agent, no longer bothered to put individual 'For Sale' signs out in front of each abandoned home. Nearly seventy per cent of the village was for sale and nobody was buying, and at the age of 77, Dan was no longer investing in fancy promotions.

On the seventeenth of July, a great roar of joy shook the cobwebs on the ceiling of the public bar of the Green Dog. Not only was Dan offering a round of drinks to all those present, but he had announced with a voice almost strangled by suppressed pride and joy, that number fourteen had just been sold. Two minutes later, anyone leaving the pub would have heard from the open upstairs window of the house across the street the familiar clickety-click of Mabel's typewriter, as she bashed out the good news. The duplicator would be running hot tonight, as the two sisters took turns spinning its handle. Tomorrow, the free Midlow Newsletter would confirm the good news.

Dan was very discreet, despite the excitement that encouraged the more ambitious to forecast a sudden economic surge in Little Midlow. Optimists saw the sign of an influx of new migrants and new businesses, the re-opening of the school, even the appearance of the village's first supermarket,The arrival at number fourteen of plumbers, electricians and painters, the appearance of tradesmen carrying carpets, furniture and curtains increased the level of excitement. Many of them lunched at the Green Dog and it was from the public bar of this fine establishment that a profile of the newcomer slowly formed.The Wrinkle sisters' next edition of the Newsletter confirmed everything that was said.

She was a widow, her name was Sarah Aghassi, and she was not related to any famous tennis player. She wanted to live in the village because it was quiet, because there was little traffic and because she found the surrounding countryside very beautiful. She lived alone with a cat called Solomon and she knew nobody in Little Midlow. According to the lady from Melbourne who had come especially to fit her curtains, she did not appear eager to make friends. As the weeks went by, little snippets were added to little snippets, and the next Newsletter provided a further update. Sarah Aghassi was the daughter of immigrants from Iran, she was a philosopher of repute in certain countries of the Middle East, and wealthy although nobody knew the origins of her fortune.

Ethel and Mabel Winkle were developing an image of the future resident that was beginning to worry those who enjoyed worrying. Was this woman a person of good reputation, or could she be involved in matters that could cause grave concern for the good citizens of Little Midlow, they asked? The recent commemoration of the anniversary of the Twin Tower disaster in New York was fresh in all minds, and while the village could hardly be considered a target of strategic importance, caution should be exercised.

We must be careful," Basil from number 26 suggested one evening in the public bar.

"She might be a friend of Al Kinder," Gregory from number 17 warned them.

The others laughed. Gregory was always a little confused about contemporary matters.

"She's certainly not some Kylie Minogue," Derek from number 8 commented. "Otherwise we would have had the press here long ago."

This provoked even more laughter. There had been a rumour going round the little village for some time that Dan Cullen had written to the pop star offering her number 6 for eighty-five thousand dollars but had received no reply. The fact that the Winkle sisters had never reported the event meant that it was probably untrue.

The removal van arrived on the 4th September. It was black, as were the uniforms of the men who unloaded the private belongings of Ms Aghassi. Its size alone caused stress in the village, and for more than an hour the main street was seriously encumbered, only pedestrians and cyclists could wiggle their way past. Ethel Winkle felt that tingling sensation in her bones, a feeling that was warning her that this was an important moment in the history of the village. She pulled her new Nikon out of its black carry bag, switched it on and began to take pictures from her attic window. The huffing and heaving, the guttural orders, muttered or even whispered, the scraping and squeaking that accompanied the progress of large objects around impossible corners or through narrow passageways provoked an unexplainable feeling of apprehension.

It was the last object to leave the van that sent a shudder of fear up many spines. It was a rectangular box of blackened wood, whose sides were about fifty centimetres high and wide, more than two metres long, and it was quietly threatening. Ethel's camera swallowed the dangerous object from every angle.

The van disappeared just before midday and a deathly silence fell on the village. There were things to be said, concerns to be expressed, fears to be aired, but nobody seemed prepared to take the first step.

Mabel Tingle was infusing a delightful Lady Grey in her Vanderbilt porcelain teapot and Ethel was slicing the Fruit and Orange Zest Cake when a car door slammed. They were in such a hurry to rush to the window that Mabel spilt some hot tea on the Irish linen table cloth and Ethel dropped a slice of cake on the polished floorboards. They arrived in time to see a large black limousine whispering its way out of the village while a little old lady in a black dress and black hat was just closing the door of the newly furnished house behind her. Sarah Aghassi had arrived, and the population of Little Midlow had just grown by 0.8 per cent in one day, an event unprecedented for more than a century.

Genteel ladies such as the Tingles do not usually frequent places of debauch, dens of pleasure, or darkened rooms where lewd gestures and vile words can be exchanged. Baby-foot, flippers, mushroom billiards and the sounds of Midnight Oil complaining about burning beds is not an environment with which they are familiar. However, that evening was special, and the two spinsters reluctantly joined the unusually large crowd of drinkers in the public bar of the Green Dog. If conclusions were to be drawn and decisions were to be taken, their sagacity would be vital.

They described in detail the goods that had arrived in the house and Ethel Winkle was proud to show off some digital pictures. The tension was such that glasses of beer were growing warm and forgotten on tables.

It was the black box that worried them all. They viewed it from all angles on the magic screen of Ethel's camera and came to a unanimous conclusion. It contained some sort of weapon, probably a device that would launch a rocket filled with dangerous substances that could poison not only the village itself but the whole region.

After two dry Sherries, a level of intoxication she had only reached once to celebrate the election of Gough Whitlam, Ethel Tingle proposed a strategy. Hat askew, cheeks flushed, she explained her contacts. The sisters had a nephew called William who worked for the government in Melbourne, who had a friend who was living with a young lady, whose brother drove a limousine in Canberra, who met people employed in buildings that sheltered activities hidden behind anonymous acronyms, and whose job was to ensure the security of the nation.

The Edward VII and Queen Alexandra Coronation Plates almost fell from the walls of the public bar with the roar of unanimous approval. Neighbours were slapping one another on the back and Mortimer Brookster from number 16 accidentally kissed Ethel on both cheeks to express his enthusiasm.

There was no debate, no hesitation. One hundred and eighty five hearts throbbed in patriotic unity. It was agreed that Ethel would call William on the telephone the following morning. By noon of that day, wheels were in motion: William had called Brian who spoke to Lizzie who texted Robert who spoke to Mr Styles who expressed concern to Lieutenant Colonel Higgins, who picked up the red phone and called ASTIC who asked for as written report in triplicate. Higgins told them to get lost and rang AMOK on the blue phone who advised the Prime Minister. That night, villagers with the most acute hearing, and they were not numerous, heard discreet rumbling and clicking in the common downhill from the village. By midnight, all lights were off and many were trembling apprehensively under their blankets.

The next morning, just after sunrise, the mist on the common cleared and six military vehicles appeared, engines roaring, banners swaying, radios crackling, as they moved determinedly towards the village. Ethel's camera was recording the event for posterity while she dictated her excited impressions to a breathless Mabel.

Suddenly the vehicles stopped, turrets moved from right to left and gun barrels were raised. A very military voice on a very powerful loudspeaker invited Ms Aghassi to surrender, hands above her head.

The appearance of the pale, frail old lady, trembling gnarled hands squeezing the tight, grey bun on her head, apron ruffling in the wind and tears streaming down her wrinkled face was a terrible anti-climax.

A deep sigh swept through the village, not of relief but of shame and of compassion.

Around noon, it seemed quite possible that military observers, journalists, camera-persons and politicians offering irrelevant commentaries outnumbered the inhabitants themselves. Major General Ducksbottom announced with unrestrained pride that yesterday's military exercise showed how both the military and the civil population could unite in times of danger.

All fears concerning Ms Aghassi were dispelled when the black box was opened in the public bar to disclose a magnificent mahogany coffin decorated with a large Cross. The villagers learned with pride that the little old lady, once a fervent member of the Armenian Apostolic Church of Iran, had fled her country of birth in 1979. She was not a terrorist, just a frightened old lady.

After her second glass of Tullamore Dew on ice, she confessed that she had moved to the village to seek peace and had brought the coffin with her to avoid any embarrassment for the shire when she died. Nobody reminded her of the numerous possibilities of funeral insurance offered on daytime commercial television, particularly by Globe Providence Insurance, but they all promised that they would attend her funeral.

Inspired by her arrival, Dan Cullen prepared a tasteful advertisement that appeared in the real estate section of the regional newspaper. It read: "Come to Little Midlow—A Peaceful Place to Die."

MARY, MARY, QUITE CONTRARY

As an agent of Globe Providence Insurance in the coastal town of Whittlewood, Malcolm was a personality. This is why he was invited to the cocktail party celebrating the opening of the town's first squash club. He hated squash because he was middle-aged and lazy and considered the sport as a form of energetic suicide. But Malcolm was at a loose end, his wife was having an affair with a man running a Kitchen Man franchise and he never refused a free drink.

When you live in a small town you are hungry for new faces, potentially new clients, so when Malcolm saw the strangers he homed in. Within two minutes he was chatting gaily to Tom and Mary. Tom was a newly appointed engineer with Rattlespoon & Leyland, and she was his young and newly appointed wife. He was a boring bespectacled Scotsman, she was tall and slim with a pretty face and a cheeky sense of humour. They were as well matched as a T-bone steak and a chocolate mousse: both interesting, but not together.

Malcolm told Tom that he had just lost a secretary and Tom told him that Mary was a secretary looking for a job. It's a small world.

"Can you type?" Malcolm asked her.

'Most secretaries do," she replied chirpily. "But only if I have to."

He grinned, realising that she was exactly the kind of person who would lighten up his boring office.

"How about shorthand?" he asked.

"The left one's shorter than the right but I get by," she bantered.

Tom intervened gruffly.

"She's a qualified short-hand typist and a good secretary," he announced firmly and in a dour, humourless tone. "She needs a job because we need the money."

Malcolm offered her the job and Tom accepted on her behalf. Malcolm sighed. There were too many Toms in this world.

They had another drink, shook hands and Malcolm gave her the office address, inviting her to start the following Monday at nine. She appeared ten minutes late and apologised with a sheepish smile.

"There's a rather nice dress shop on the ground floor," she explained. "It caught my attention."

He nodded but reminded her that punctuality was the mother of courtesy or something similar and they spent the next hour wandering around the office looking at her new headquarters. She loved the coffee machine, was delighted with the Olympia electric typewriter and was thrilled that her office had a big window looking over the square.

"Three months here will be wonderful," she declared happily over a cup of coffee and a Tim Tam.

"Three months?"

"Yes, well I am only doing this because Tom has some settling-in expenses, afterwards I want to have time to do my shopping, meet new friends, you know what I mean."

Malcolm was annoyed by the announcement but decided to let the matter slip. As the weeks went by, she settled in and became, very quickly, an ideal colleague. Her typing was fast and neat, she was an excellent stenographer, she loved to chat about nothing important and all the friends and clients who walked in to the office were delighted. A few of them even whispered an envious 'lucky bastard!' in Malcolm's ear.

Winter disappeared, spring showers brought out the blossoms and the date of that proposed departure grew inexorably closer. Discreetly, Malcolm rang Tom and he accepted with obvious enthusiasm his invitation to lunch. They met at the Golden Spoon, Malcolm chose the chicken pie while Tom opted for the fish and chips.

"I wanted to talk about Mary," Malcolm explained.

Tom grunted and, not sure of what that meant, Malcolm pressed on.

"I was rather hoping she could stay on, but she seems decided to leave at the end of three months."

"Maybe if you offered her more money she would," Tom suggested through a mouthful of battered flake. "Money's always a good incentive."

"It might be a little early for that," Malcolm parried. "Let's give her time to settle down."

"She never does," Tom commented.

"She's efficient and competent, and it's not easy to find those qualities in a secretary in our little town," Malcolm explained.

"Are you sure? That doesn't sound like her," Tom commented with a surprised look on his face. A forkful of soggy chips had stopped in mid-air, about an inch from his mouth.

How could Malcolm tell him that she brought joy into his office and his life, that she was the main reason he rushed to work every day, heart beating, a spring in his step? How do you tell a dour husband that he is bloody lucky to have such a charming, cheerful and pretty wife?

"Look," Tom said waving the forkful of chips in his direction," I want her to be in a full time, permanent job, earning good money and not wandering around town with my credit card."

"Maybe you should tell her," Malcolm suggested. "Gently, diplomatically, so that she understands your financial problems."

"What financial problems?" Tom shouted loudly. "Who told you I had financial problems?"

People from nearby tables looked up with worried expressions on their faces. A waiter stopped, turned towards them, asking himself if trouble was brewing. Concern distorted his face.

"I'm sorry, it's not want I meant," Malcolm replied quietly.

Reluctantly, Malcolm offered her an extra forty dollars a fortnight. Reluctantly, Mary accepted and stayed on. Gradually, she began to enjoy her job and his company. He noticed that month after month she was becoming more elegant, more attractive, more amusing. She loved to organise his schedule of appointments and enjoyed the little secrets of the business. She also took a genuine professional interest in what he or rather they achieved. He began to realise that she was no longer an accessory, but an indispensable partner.

He was no longer the agent of the firm, they were an agency. And it was good fun, too!

He was sitting at home one evening listening to his wife chatting on the phone, sipping a glass of whisky and pretending to watch a programme on TV about Panda bears.

"Oh, Roger, what a great idea," his other half giggled. "I'll get changed and meet you in an hour in front of the Hot Spot."

She hung up and turned to him.

"I'm going to a new night club with Roger and his wife," she announced happily before running upstairs to put on something totally inappropriate but which was supposed to make her look younger.

"Roger got divorced six months ago," he replied, but she was already round the bend in the staircase. "His wife moved to Sydney."

"You were probably the reason, "he added very quietly so that she could not hear.

He knew that there would be no point waiting up for her to come home.

"Roger is so charming, and funny, and such a good dancer," she told him about three times a week.

Roger was also twenty-eight and drove a Stag.

There was only one drawback in the office. Although theirs was a nice little town, Mary was homesick for Melbourne, Sunday lunches with Mum and Dad, a round of golf with her brother, shopping in Southland, and the noise and bustle of a big city. She left him twice, tossing the keys of her office on the desk to say she was going home. Each time he rang Tom to tell him that she was parked on Browne Bluff and that if he was not there within half an hour to talk to her in a positive way she was going to leave him. He did not add and, more importantly, she would leave the agency as well.

Each time she came back in the afternoon, blushing beautifully to ask if he had any letters to type, as if nothing had happened. He could have hugged her each time but she was young, sweet, eighteen years younger than him and irretrievably married.

When he told her one morning that he was taking a couple of hours off to move into a small furnished flat because he was leaving his wife, she was delighted. Theirs was a small town, and even Mary, a relative newcomer, had caught up with the rumours. As they were closing the office that evening, she announced with great determination that she was taking him down to the supermarket to make sure that he had everything he needed.

Obediently, he pushed the trolley from aisle to aisle, watching it fill: toothpaste, canned asparagus, toilet rolls, milk, a chicken, a toilet brush, two packets of cream biscuits, instant coffee, towels, dish-washing detergent, baked beans, tea towels, laundry powder, a TV guide, three frozen dinners, glasses, liquid soap, jam, bed linen, a bottle of white wine, bread, shampoo, cheese . . . it never seemed to stop.

The check-out chick smiled approvingly.

"Looking after your Dad, are you?" she asked.

Malcolm glared.

"Why don't you just do your job without asking stupid questions." he muttered angrily.

Mary patted his arm to calm him down.

"He's a good friend and he's just left his wife," she explained gently. "He's a bit sensitive at the moment."

The girl blushed.

"I'm sorry and good luck," she told him. "It looks as if you are in good hands."

Mary insisted on coming home, packing everything away and showing him how to use the oven, the cook top, the microwave, and the rubbish bin, before making the bed. They then shared a glass of wine to drink a toast to his new-found freedom and he suggested that Tom might be wondering where she was.

"He's in Brisbane," she announced happily. "He won't be back until Thursday. You can take me out to dinner to thank me for the help you know. Shopping is not on my duty statement."

He grinned happily and took her to a pizzeria. When they got back to his place she climbed out of the car, smiling happily.

"Would you like me to spend the night here?" she asked. "It could be quite intimidating, your first night alone."

He was still gasping for air when she added.

"You do have a spare bedroom, don't you?"

His heart slowed to about 180 while he assured he would be perfectly safe alone. She gave him a little peck on the cheek before climbing into her Spitfire and he wondered quietly if there would ever, ever be a more wonderful moment in his life.

She came to work one day wearing what he would call a 'peasant' blouse. It's a blouse with an elastic top that uncovers the shoulders. Only Mary could choose to wear something sexy and look embarrassed. He invited her into his office and began to dictate letters and saw she was looking for flattering comments.

Being Mary, she began to giggle and jiggle, and the top began to slip down, ever so slowly.

"I think the elastic is a little loose," she said with a shy little laugh.

He stood up and walked around the desk.

"I'll have a look," He suggested.

He stood behind her and slipped his hands under the elastic. Her eyes were closed and her lips began to tremble. He slipped his hands further down to cup a small naked breast in each. Her eyes were still closed and her cheeks were red. Neither of them spoke or moved for a couple of minutes.

"I'll have to tighten the elastic top" she whispered suddenly, with a deep sigh. "Are they adequate?"

"Adequate is a good word," he assured her as he withdrew his hands and pulled the top back into place.

She wore that top several times afterwards, above all the days when he announced that tomorrow there was a lot of mail to dictate, but he stayed firmly on his side of the desk. She giggled as it slid down, very, very slowly, but he continued steadfastly to dictate the mail.

The second great surprise when she arrived one morning, rushing into his office and closing the door behind her.

"Tom made love to me last night!" she announced excitedly.

Malcolm was dumbfounded.

She did make another bad mistake, just once. They received a visit from a gruff Regional Controller of the Firm, one of those routine checks which seem to only aim at humiliating those who strive to serve a cause with honesty and determination.

He was talking to Malcolm when she brought in two cups of coffee.

"Your girl takes shorthand, I understand?" he asked gruffly. "Could she do a short letter for me?"

She smiled sweetly as she placed his cup on the desk.

"Sorry, Jack, I've already done one letter today," she said, intending to joke.

Jack did not share her sense of humour and said as much quite bluntly and she was very red-faced as she sat beside him, pencil and pad in hand.

An invitation arrived a week later in the mail. This time Malcolm was invited to a cocktail party celebrating the opening of a new hotel in the town centre. He hated new hotels, but decided to attend.

"The invitation is for Mr and Mrs" Mary pointed out.

He shrugged his shoulders.

"Tell them there is no longer a missus and I'll come alone," he told her.

The day of the cocktail party she took the afternoon off. Malcolm was at home getting dressed for the event when the doorbell rang. He gasped when he opened the door. Mary had obviously been to a beautician and her make-up was absolutely perfect. Her hair was lifted into a little curly pig tail at the back and she had delightful ear rings, little hoops on a gold chain. She was wearing a long clinging dress of pale grey silk hanging on her shoulders by two very thin straps. The cleavage was enticing without being vulgar.

"I forget to tell them there was no longer a missus so I thought I'd come along," she announced with a cheeky grin.

When they reached the lobby of the hotel he actually heard the noisy conversations die away. There was a stunned silence for a couple of minutes, and then the conversations picked up again. When he introduced her to various acquaintances as 'my secretary' some smiled like clowns, some even sniggered.

"You're not ashamed of me, are you," she whispered shyly over her second glass of wine.

"Don't be silly," he whispered back. "I think you're magnificent tonight and the firm should be proud of you. Even Jack."

As they left, Michelle, a little blonde divorcee who had been fluttering her eyelashes in Malcolm's direction for a few weeks, was coming up the stairs towards them. She gaped at his stunning companion and stumbled. He actually heard Mary chuckle with delight.

"Silly little tart," she hissed between clenched teeth.

As they climbed into his car, she told him that she believed that after a cocktail party the tradition was that the gentleman took the lady out for dinner. She suggested that it was usually something expensive, discreet, a little tête-à-tête in a nice restaurant with fine food and exquisite wines. He agreed and rang Tom to ask him to join them. He refused bluntly, as he was in the process of rebuilding a lawnmower. He took her to his favourite place, *Chez Victor*, and Georges, a waiter from Nouméa who had joined Bernadette and Gaston a few months ago, was very impressed.

"She's much prettier than your ex-wife," he commented in French as he was serving two flutes of champagne.

"*Merci*," she chirped.

Malcolm had forgotten that she had done French with the Sisters of the Immaculate Conception in Oakleigh. He blushed and Georges laughed and winked.

"I'm sorry about that," he apologised when Georges finally left us.

She assured him that she had been flattered by the compliment. They had a delightful evening and when Georges escorted them to the door he paid her another compliment.

"It is always a pleasure to serve a beautiful woman who appreciates good food," he said in English and with a bow.

"I'm sure it must be," she said, with a cheeky twinkle in her eye.

As the door closed behind them they left Georges with a frown on his face, wondering what to make of the reply.

In December Mary stormed into Malcolm's office, obviously in a bad mood, threw the keys to her office on his desk and announced her immediate departure. Obviously, Tom was in trouble, again. Malcolm stood up, pulled his own key ring from my pocket and tossed it on the desk beside hers.

"I'm coming with you," he announced firmly.

She froze, gaped at him in surprise, and then she laughed.

"That would be super," she announced.

He whisked a few personal belongings into his brief case and they left. Before they got into the lift, she stuck a short typed note on the office door. 'We've gone away, signed Malcolm and Mary', it said.

They packed a suitcase each which they tossed into the back of the Discovery and left her Spitfire in the office car park. A few hours later they were sitting side by-side in the setting sun on a quiet beach, sharing a bottle of chilled white wine and a bag of battered scallops. Slowly, shyly, his hand crept across the sand towards her until their fingers touched. She grabbed it and turned towards him to kiss him lightly on the cheek.

"It'll only be for three months," she whispered. "And we'll just be friends,"

He nodded.

"But it will be good fun," he replied wistfully

He knew already that in three months she would be going back to dour, humourless Tom. She had been brought up by an old-fashioned Catholic family, and she had old-fashioned principles.

GEORGE, CHANTAL, TED AND THE TECHNICAL REVOLUTION

George was a little surprised.

"Where's this come from?" he asked Chantal. "Has the boss gone mad?"

Chantal shook her head.

"I've never seen it before. I think it's crazy to introduce another brand of washing machine. We have too many, already. And this is Blaxford, not Chadstone!"

"It's the franchiser's decision, a novelty item," Ted concluded." Unless it's something fallen off the back of a Korean truck."

The Great Mates Store in Blaxford was big. George reckoned that on some winter mornings, the girls at the sales desk could hardly see the other end of the store through the fog. But the new machine would be visible from afar.

Chantal rang up Josie who worked for the Great Mates franchise in Sutton Vale.

"We've got one here too," she announced. "It's a Daipong Hydramatic!"

Ted was probably right. The brand name, Daipong, sounded Korean.

"I bet they also make container ships, mobile phones, china tea sets, fighter aircraft, land mines, inflatable dolls and plasma TV sets," he surmised.

Chantal giggled.

"That's what happens, in those 'emerging economies'", George explained knowingly.

Josie's boss, Ted, and their boss, Chris, like all the other Great Mates franchisees were attending a seminar organised by some expensive consultants in an unknown venue in a secret location somewhere near Surfers Paradise. They familiarised themselves with new products, they 'bonded' they did funny drawings on butcher's paper, they chased one another through forests with paint guns, they learned about game plans and they switched off their mobiles phones. The staff in Blaxford, as did the guys in Ashmeadow, Newbridge and Whittlewood, came to the conclusion that while the bosses were all playing silly buggers, the top brass had decided to launch a new brand.

George, Chantal and Ted opened the Blaxford store on Monday morning, and the usual trickle of customers appeared. Most Great Mates customers came to replace something that was broken or obsolete, and started with a modest budget. They usually left half an hour later with something they could not afford or with something completely different.

The store knew its customers well. They usually lived in big empty homes with a built-in five star kitchen in Albanian Maple and Nepalese Granite. Most of them had three cars, a forty-year mortgage and credit, savings, cheque, fast-draw and easy access accounts with five different banks. Furnishings were often limited to mattresses on the floor, beanbags and two or three plasma TV's. When Basher and Highfull brought out a new fridge, Mum and Dad were in the store, waving their brand new platinum credit card and shouting for same-day delivery.

This Monday was different. This was to be the first day of the Daipong era. Whatever the Barringtons, the Smiths, the Mappersons, the Waddles and all the others came in to buy that day, they all left with a new Daipong Hydramatic washing machine.

"I don't believe it," Chantal whispered to Ted."They just ignore me and go straight to the new washing machine. It's scary!"

That day the store sold eighteen of them and nothing else. George was terrified. As each family entered through the main door, the Daipong Hydramatic lit up, its control board began to flash and it started to beep. All the customers were immediately attracted to the machine and stood around it as if in a dazed while it twinkled and burped at them.

How does it do that?" he asked Chantal. It's not even connected to the power!"

At the end of the day, George, Chantal and Ted closed up, quite pale-faced.

The next morning, George came in very early to open up the store. He stopped near the cash registers, hit the lights switch and stood still, eyes bulging, heart pounding. Much of the traditional stock had disappeared overnight, replaced by new Daipong products. Steam irons, toasters, sandwich makers, kitchen robots, three-speed mixers, kettles, fat-free grills and electric woks had all appeared as if by magic. Yet nobody had opened the building overnight.

Once the lights were on they all began to chatter, warble and flash, yet not one of them had a plug connected to a power source. Large Daipong banners hung from the ceiling and a compact CD player began playing a song they would soon know by heart and hate: the Daipong jingle.Yet the safety locks had remained intact and Eric Chapman, the manager of the company charged with ensuring overnight security swore that there had been no strange movements recorded.

When Chantal and Ted arrived they found George pale, his hands shaking. He was very, very frightened.

"Look at the shop, look at the shop!" he babbled, gesticulating wildly. They looked, and understood his fear.

He sent an E-mail to six or seven other franchised stores across Victoria, asking 'what the hell was going on?' but saw his messages rejected within a few minutes. Mail Demon told him that all internal messages should be limited to business matters. He then received a personal message from Public Relations in Head Office, warning him that comments about Daipong over the intranet system should only be flattering.

Realising that the surveillance cameras were probably recording their conversations, George, Chantal and Ted withdrew into the toilet area and with two Daipong hair-dryers switched on at full speed, they discussed their future.

"Why don't we close the shop and go home?" Chantal suggested. "We'll wait for Chris to come back from his seminar."

George shook his head.

"I reckon the shop will open itself and run everything without us," he said glumly.

The others agreed. After a day of record sales to customers who all appeared to be in a state of advanced hypnosis, they all went home and from the privacy of their own dwelling, and, following Ted's bright idea, they called other members of the nation-wide Great Mates franchise, all listed on the social club annual registry.

By the end of the evening, they had discovered that the same range of Daipong products was sitting on the floor of stores across five States. In fact, Daipong was the only brand in all of their stores. Sales, they learned, were going through the roof.

The next strange event was the disappearance of the franchisees. According to a Great Mates newsletter, at the end of the seminar they had decided unanimously to sell out their businesses and retire. Luckily, Great Mates and Daipong had buyers hovering in the background.

George went round to see Chris that evening, because they had all considered him not just as a boss, but a mate; a Great Mate, in fact. However, when he rang the bell, a very agitated Angela begged him tearfully to go away, assuring him that Chris was very happy and that they were all moving to a retirement village in Vanuatu. All the curtains were drawn and the cat was tearing at the fly screen door, trying to get in.

Within a few days, private phone calls through the social club network confirmed that, like Chris, Ted, Johnny, Steve, Mike, Roger the Dodger, Wally Walbrook and all the others had retired. They were all going to live in the same retirement village, and they all had a new set of Daipong golf clubs.

The following Monday, Victor, the new manager of the Blaxford store arrived. He was tall, gaunt, with a grey-green skin, big black eyes and he never smiled. He wore a black suit and a black tie and slid noiselessly around the shop on black leather shoes. Photos and messages exchanged by personal mobile phone quickly confirmed that all the other stores had a manager called Victor and they all looked identical.

Thursday, a new sales executive arrived in the store. Her name was Vanessa, and she was the manager's niece. She stood at the entrance of the shop and greeted each visitor with the same message with a voice that sounded as if it had been pre-recorded on a Mixmaster. She wore a silver mini-dress, silver boots and a sparkling diadem. Her body looked as if it had just come out of a swimsuit catalogue, but her hair was green.

"Welcome to Great Mates," she hissed, mouth breaking into a commercial smile and red eyes sparkling. "Choose your next Daipong product carefully, it could earn you rewards and discounts on your next purchase."

The visitors never seemed to know what they wanted.

"I can't remember why I came here," one elderly lady moaned.

"You're looking for the automatic toaster," Vanessa assured her, gently pushing her in the right direction.

Poor old Mr Ferguson, who was at least eighty, seemed exceptionally excited when Vanessa whispered something in his ear.

"I've always wanted a fridge with a TV in the door," he giggled on his way out.

"It will be delivered tomorrow," Vanessa assured him, squeezing his arm reassuringly.

Friday, George, Chantal and Ted learned that they were no longer 'sales executives' but 'operating agents' and as such would be required to sweep, mop and polish the floors and clean the windows every day.

Mr Starvey, reputed businessman and partner in Starvey and Foreman, appeared on Today Tonight to announce that they were closing eighteen stores across Australia and putting off two hundred staff. He added that their demise was due to unfair and invasive competition. His body was found two days later on the eleventh green of the Blue Haven Golf Course and it was announced that he had committed suicide by attempting to swallow his Daipong putter.

On 14 August, Blaxford store's M. Victor's left arm fell off and two customers fainted. He quickly slipped it back up into the sleeve of his suit where it clicked into place immediately. On 11 September, The Sutton Vale shop's Mr Victor's head popped off while he was demonstrating a coffee grinder. Two elderly clients left horizontally, in an ambulance, and without making a purchase. The head was fitted back into place quite easily, but one eye glowed green for several hours before burning out. On 14 November, in the middle of a massive promotion in the Whittlewood store, the resident Mr Victor exploded, causing harm to several bystanders.

There was obviously a problem with the new generation of store managers, and all Mr. Victors were withdrawn from service on 18 November for a three-day check-up. A staff bulletin announced a revival seminar, but there were rumours among staff concerning faulty fuses, chipped microchips and men doing things with screwdrivers and curses.

Fortunately, a new generation of Victors was back on duty, nation-wide, for the great Christmas promotion. All Great Mate stores were going to offer the Daipong Diarama eight-foot wide plasma TV, for only $29. 95.

Customers were fighting to get into a Great Mates store. Credit cards nearly reached melting point. The word was out. Any bloke who did not have an eight-foot Diarama in his home for Christmas would probably see his wife, kids and dog leave the house. Social services were on the alert, Mothers-in-Law Anonymous set up a 24-hour emergency call-in service.

The great novelty with the Diarama was that it did not need an aerial. It came with a clothes hoist for the back yard that included a tiny satellite dish that picked up more than sixty channels with only subliminal advertising that never interfered with programs. Suddenly life became happy, carefree, and pleasurable.

"Humanity adapts to all new forms of rubbish," Ted sighed. "I give up. Nobody worries, nobody cares and the younger generation thinks it's normal to be treated like imbeciles."

Chantal was secretly unhappy, but kept her thoughts to herself. Her husband and the kids loved their new Daiwhatever life, where a new gimmick arrived every month to please them. But George was finally victim of the stress. One morning, just after the opening, he threw himself at the new Daipong refrigerator that had arrived, axe brandished over his head, screaming threats in a language that sounded Japanese. His gesture was frozen by a beam from Mr Victor's left forefinger, and he now stands in front of the shop as a concrete acknowledgement of Daipong technology. Children laugh at him and dogs pee on his left leg.

By Easter, Chantal and Ted were wondering why there had been so much fuss and stress. Their salaries had doubled, they were allowed four cups of tea a day with, for the first time in their career, chocolate biscuits, and they enjoyed an eighty per cent discount on any article in the store. Admittedly, Mr Victor had occasional problems with his circuits, but whenever he began to smoke, burble or crackle an emergency unit with screwdriver and spare eardrum appeared within a few minutes.

"I reckon it's the English Breakfast Tea," Chantal suggested. "They should serve him warm sewing machine oil, he'd feel much better."

Finally, Ted cracked. A black van from the new State Department of Absolute Peace appeared and three men took him away, screaming about civil liberties, workers' rights, free choice, twenty/twenty cricket and sick leave. There was a rumour circulating around the other shops that he had joined a terrorist group that deliberately sabotaged Mr Victors around the country. Chantal laughed.

"You've got to sway with the wind," she told her husband one day during a Daipong staff picnic. "I bet Ted is in a retirement village somewhere."

"Probably playing lawn bowls up in Noosa," her husband suggested. "Here, have another snag."

But Chantal knew that he didn't believe it. Electronic Euphoria comes at a price; and that price is silence.

NEW FRIENDS

"More bloody cards," Daniel moaned, tossing the mail on the dining room table.

From afar, Ethel recognised a bill from the water board, a letter from their local politician, an appeal from a charity and a brochure from Great Mates. Admittedly, there were the usual square and coloured enveloped offering season's greetings and recommending good health.

"We just have to check them off against the list," she reminded her husband.

Daniel and Ethel had a safety system. They listed all the cards they had already sent out, to make sure that senders were automatically receivers and nobody was offended. 'Thrust and parry', Ethel called it. Her husband said she was a cynic and she agreed.

"I remember four years ago when Dad had a terminal cancer the number of cards he received wishing him good health for the coming year. Most people feel they are obliged to send cards, very few actually do it with sincere friendship and goodwill."

Daniel sighed, agreeing with his wife, and, without too much enthusiasm, they began to open the new cards, taking a small pile each.

"Here's one from Tom and Jane," Ethel announced. "Their son's got the sack again."

Tom grunted.

"Sophie and Marie are off to Thailand," he announced. "A honeymoon, they say."

"That's the third," Ethel commented.

They continued opening more cards, announcing greetings from Harvey, Tom and Barbara, the Atkinson family and Brian and his new wife.

"Oh dear," Ethel called out. "Here's one with one of those 'what we did this year' letters inside."

"I thought that went out of fashion, "Daniel replied. "Who's it from?"

"Trevor and Deirdre," she replied.

Daniel frowned.

"Who are they? I don't think we know any Trevor and Deirdre."

Ethel looked at the envelope.

"They're from Sutton Vale. Oh dear, I shouldn't have opened it, it was for the Watsons."

Daniel and Ethel had bought their house from the Watson family just ten months ago.

Daniel laughed.

"Let's read it anyway. It could be good fun."

Ethel nodded happily.

"They've put their address on the back of the envelope so we can send them a card back. That'll get them guessing!"

"They might recognise the address," Daniel suggested.

Ethel shrugged her shoulders.

"Who cares? I'll make a cup of tea and we'll read the Trevor and Deirdre story."

With Earl Grey teabags infusing in Sovereign Hill mugs and a plate of Ginger Nuts in front of them, they began to read. It said:

'Dear Friends,

Well another year has gone by, the months seem to fly by so quickly as you get older, but luckily Trevor keeps a diary so we can tell you about all the exciting things that have happened to us this year. Our son Ian had a ski accident in Thredbo this winter and was on crutches for two months. Our eldest daughter, Allison, is still working with the mission group in the Solomon Islands and has a new boyfriend. She sent us a photo of herself with the new partner and his four kids. He is a local man, quite dark, but she says he is very good to her. She wants to bring them over to meet us next year, and I wonder what the neighbours will think. Aunt Betty flew down from Surfers to visit us at Easter, she stayed for eight days and moaned every day about the cold weather. Apparently she won forty five thousand dollars in a jackpot at Jupiter's, but she only invited us out once, to KFC.

In August, Trevor went to the Kiwanis International Convention in Adelaide, and he gave a talk about the history of postage stamps in Australia. I (Deirdre) stayed at home because I had to look after two grandchildren while their mother, Robert's wife, was having another baby. It is a boy and they have christened him Bentley Weston. Caroline, the mother, is a snob so we all call the baby Benny just to annoy her.

We spent eighteen days in Europe this year in September and visited Italy, France and Spain. We saw everything and most of you would have received the photo we sent by email of Trevor standing in front of the Eiffel Tower. This year we are going to the U.K. To visit my family as well as Ireland where Trevor has some cousins he hasn't seen in thirty years. We will be away for eight weeks, during next summer so if anyone wants to use our holiday home in Cockatoo Reach for a week or so, please let us know.

As for the rest of the family news, it was as pretty mixed bag. Trevor's brother Eric got divorced, my sister Ethel had her appendix removed, our third son Bill has joined the Army and Trevor's niece Betty has been sent to Uruguay as a Trade Commissioner, whatever that is.

Hugs to you from us, Trevor & Deirdre.

"I wonder why people inflict their pathetic news on their friends," Ethel said, when they had finished laughing, as she screwed up the letter into a ball.

"Hey wait a minute!" Daniel called out, grabbing her arm. "Didn't we say we were going to reply?"

Ethel frowned.

"Why would we do that?'

"I'll explain tomorrow," Daniel said with a grin.

The next morning, Ethel chose a nice card out of their Salvation Army collection and wrote a kind Christmas message to Deirdre and Trevor from Daniel and Ethel. Inside the card was one of those boring letters that people inflict on their friends every year. Daniel had prepared it with care. It read:

Dear Trevor & Deirdre,

I was SO happy to receive your card and your letter. We hope you have a lovely Christmas. Trevor and I had a good time at the convention in Adelaide, his talk about postage stamps went straight to my heart as I am an avid collector, and I remember with delight the chats we had over a few beers some evenings. I am very flattered to know that he remembered me, yes I'm Daniel, the guy who had a collection of stamps illustrating famous battleships.

Unlike you, we did not get away this year for a holiday. While I was in Adelaide my wife, Ethel, broke a leg, and in October our dog Gainsborough was taken sick and died.

The year had already got away to a bad start. In February, Our eldest son, Hannibal, was captured by pirates when sailing with friends off the coast of Malaysia, and we had to pay an important ransom to get him back. In April my Renault 25 died of old age so we now only have Ethel's old Kingswood Ute to get around. In November, Ethel caught the exotic cheekenkormar virus which is caught by licking empty fast food containers. She had been very brave putting up with the four daily injections in her buttocks but she is very pale and has lost a lot of weight. The doctor thinks that a couple of months by the sea would do her good. She needs to feel the sun on her cheeks, let the sea breeze play with her long golden hair and wiggle her poor, misshapen toes in the warm sand. Unfortunately, the water heater has just blown up so there will be no seaside holiday this year.

The good news is that we are now exchanging cards and I am sure we will have much better news next year. Meanwhile, if you have the time to give me a call, my mobile phone number is on the back of the card. A friendly voice warms the cockles of the heart.

Hugs, Ethel and Daniel.

Daniel and Ethel had a very heated dispute about the letter. She said that nobody could be stupid enough to believe all that rubbish, and Daniel said 'You watch!'

Trevor rang a week later. He remembered Daniel very well although he was still wondering how he could have sent him a Christmas card when he did not have his address in his address book. Daniel told him not to worry, it must have been a gift from God and he was delighted to hear Trevor's voice again.

"I never told Ethel about some of the things you and I got up to in Adelaide," Daniel whispered to his new found friend.

"Not a word to the General!" Trevor chortled while desperately trying to remember what wicked deeds they may have committed.

The following Christmas, Daniel and Ethel chose a very expensive card for their good friends from Sutton Vale. It included the traditional newsletter and Trevor was probably delighted to know that Ethel was on the mend, mainly thanks to the wonderful two months she had spent with her husband in Cockatoo Reach, in that lovely holiday home Trevor hand lent them.

True friendship is priceless.

A TRIP DOWN MEMORY LANE

Privately, Bill had to admit to himself that Lorna was right. As a man who had been a driver with Maverton Haulage for nearly thirty years, he should have been able to fix the camper car. His excuse was that modern vehicles do not break down. In the old days, when Bill was young, you changed spark plugs and ignition coils, you changed con rod bearings and spent a few hours grinding valves because that's the way things were. Twenty years ago, when cars were made by fallible humans, wheel bearings were three a penny, and if you really wanted to play a dirty trick on a mate, you pinched his rotor arm.

Today, camper cars came with five year warranty, five year roadside assistance, eight air bags, fixed rate serviced and navigation systems with sexy voices.

"So you don't know why it's stopped, you don't know where we are, and your mobile phone doesn't work," Lorna groaned. "We should never have come to Tasmania and we should never have bought the camper. We should have gone to visit the kids in Oregon."

Bill grunted. He hated flying and he hated Oregon and he hated the U.S. of A. He was looking for inspiration under the raised bonnet.

"They hide everything under these bloody plastic covers," he complained. "I can't even see the distributor."

"Maybe they don't have distributors nowadays," Lorna replied sarcastically. "They've done away with everything else."

Bill sighed wistfully.

"Remember the Rover 90. Now that was a real car . . .'

"I'll make a cup of tea," Lorna decided, opening the door of the van. "You can remember the registration of your beloved Rover 90, but you can't remember your grandchildren's first names."

Bill snorted angrily.

"That's because they're American, heathen names. And I can remember, so you're wrong. There's Brooklyn named after a bridge, Riley named after a motor car and Madison named after a dance! What's wrong with Mary, Anne or Susan, for God's sake?"

"They could have called one of them 'Lorna'," Lorna said wistfully, before disappearing inside the van.

As she prepared a pot of Darjeeling and a plate of home-made cakes, she thought about Bill. He had not been the same since he left Maverton Haulage when the new owners, he called them 'the wogs', had taken over. Since his retirement, old colleagues had whispered to him about secret compartments in some of the trucks and scheduled meetings on quiet roads with people driving white vans and wearing wrap-around sunglasses. Because he enjoyed driving, he had taken up part-time work with a smaller company delivering firewood in winter. It kept him active and it kept him out of her way. The camper van was a means of taking to the highways together.

"Do you want to put the chairs and the table under the tree?" Lorna called out when the tray with teapot, milk jug, cups and cakes was ready.

There was no reply. She called out again, but there was still no answer from Bill. Lorna put down the tray and climbed down out of the van. Bill was standing with his back to her, gazing out over the nearby meadow. She sensed something unusual, there was tenseness in his shoulders that she did not recognise. She walked towards him and placed a hand around his waist.

He jumped and shrugged her off, almost violently.

"Do you remember Aunt Muriel's funeral in Hamilton?' he asked.

She frowned.

"Of course I do. But why are you talking about funerals on such a lovely day?"

"They buried her in a family gave, with her parents and her sister," he reminded her.

She shook her head impatiently.

"I know that!"

"I never forget that dreadful sound when they slid back that big slab to open the vault," he told her sadly.

"There must be more pleasant subjects of conversation when you are in the middle of a Tasmanian wilderness," she suggested almost teasingly.

He ignored her comment.

"I have just heard that sound again," he added. "Right here, in the middle of nowhere, I heard the noise of stone rubbing against stone, just like that slab."

She stepped forward, grabbed his arm and tried to swing him round to face her. He resisted strongly but she noted that his face was dreadfully pale.

"Listen!" he hissed. "Just shut up and listen!"

She slipped her arm through his and stood beside him, realising that there was something that was really disturbing him. Tom was inclined to get up tight about little things now and again and it was best to ride out the storm quietly and wait for the bashful apology that usually followed.

Then she heard the sound.

He was right. It was exactly the sound made by a marble or granite slab sliding slowly over stone. Just like a slab sliding painfully across the walls of a family vault. It brought back memories of odours of sweet decomposition, humidity and cold. She shivered.

Suddenly, Bill pointed to the field next to the road, probably used at one time for pasture, now apparently abandoned. There was movement, tall grasses falling down as if they were being crushed by a sliding slab.

"Let's get out of here, Bill," Lorna whispered.

"We can't. The van won't start, remember?" he reminded her.

"We can walk. We'll surely meet somebody on the road who will give us a lift," she protested nervously. "I'm scared, Bill."

"We've been here for more than an hour and have not seen one car," Bill said. "In any case, I want to see what's happening. I am going to see what's in that field. If you're scared, lock yourself in the van."

She clutched his arm, begging him to stay with her but he shrugged her hand away and took a step forward. Suddenly, a beam of translucent green light seemed to emerge from the ground in the field, there where the grasses had folded. As the grinding noise continued, the beam of light grew wider.

As they stared, two small heads appeared.

"You must be Bill and Lorna," a chirpy little voice with an Irish accent announced. It had such a shy and friendly tone that Lorna's heartbeat slowed considerably. A few seconds later, two small men appeared and walked across the field towards them. They looked like characters out of a children's fantasy film. They both wore tall, black, shiny, pointed black hats with a gold buckle on the front. They wore green felt jackets, knee length, closed with big brass buttons and held by a black belt with another brass buckle. The feet and legs were enclosed in fawn coloured leather boots, and each boot had a brass buckle on the front.

Bill could not prevent himself from giggling.

"Ah, that's better," said one of the little men. "I'm Tim and this is my brother Tom, unless it's the other way around. I can never remember."

Even Lorna was smiling now.

"Well you seem to know who we are, goodness knows how, and I'm Lorna," she explained. "And because I've been married more than thirty years with this hulk, I know that his name is Bill."

Lorna noticed that they had identical faces, with brown weather-worn skin, green eyes and peaky noses.

"You look like brothers," she added.

The same little man spoke while the other nodded. They could not have been more than four feet high.

That's right," he said. "We needed to meet you so we made you come up this road and made your car stop."

"How did you do that?" Bill asked. "And which one of you is Tom? I bet you really know, don't you?"

"Questions, questions," the spokesman said testily. "We just threw a spell; it's very easy, really. And Tom is the smaller of the two. We are told that Tom measures four and a half sprockles, and Tim four and a quarter."

"So you must bed Tim," Lorna concluded. "What's a sprockle?"

Tim sighed and Tom nodded happily.

"Questions, questions, why don't you stop the questions? A sprockle is about eleven and a half woggles and a woggle is about 2.682 centimetres in your new language. It's about the same as an old Irish measure called the inch."

Bill appraised the two little men.

"That sounds about right," he concluded. "So what do we do now?"

"You follow me and stop asking questions?" Tim replied. "Come on, we're going to show you a magic world."

"Is it dangerous?" Lorna asked nervously.

"No more questions!" Tim shouted angrily. "Do I look dangerous?"

"Not really," Bill concluded. "And, by the way, that's a question."

They all laughed together and when the little men laughed it was like the tinkling of tiny bells.

Tim took Laura's hand, Tom took Bill's, or maybe it was the other way round, and they walked together towards the beam of green light coming out of the ground. Everything was suddenly very peaceful. The long grass waved gently in the soft breeze, little white clouds slid slowly across a pale blue sky, and the world was silent. As they approached, Laura and Bill realise that the opening in the ground from which the light emerged was like a large mouth, made entirely of an unusual green, translucent material. It shimmered and glowed in the soft sunlight. Neither of them felt any apprehension in being led into the strange cavern.

Once inside, their guides released their hands and they all stood for a moment, side by side, examining their surroundings. The floor, the walls and the roof of the cave seemed to be of made of uneven blocks of jade, assembled perhaps by some prehistoric upheaval.

"What do you feel, Lorna?" Bill asked his wife.

"Peace," she replied.

He laughed.

"Well, that doesn't seem to happen very often," he said teasingly. "You always seem to be running here, running there, and now you find peace when you stop running around."

"Maybe that's because you're never at home," Lorna suggested.

Bill frowned thoughtfully. Tim smiled and beckoned.

"Come with us. See that tall silver cup in the middle of the floor. It's your historical junk yard."

The silver cup was about six feet tall and seemed to be studded with blue stones. Under Tim's instructions, they formed a circle around it, holding hands: Tim, Lorna, Tom and Bill. Lorna felt her skin prickle as if there was electricity in the air.

"Ready?" Tim asked.

Lorna and Bill nodded.

Suddenly, soft music seemed to come out of the walls of the cavern, sweet, gentle music plucked on a harp. It was not loud, but it penetrated the soul. Bill and Lorna both shivered. Then a beam of soft white light appeared from the cup and tiny objects emerged, rising slowly. Although they were very small, they were quite recognisable.

There was an old Singer sowing machine, a deck of cards, an old fuel cooker, a game of Monopoly, a Mickey Mouse apron, a small and worn billiard table, a very battered red suitcase, a Sigma Station Wagon, a bag of golf clubs, an old pressure cooker, a black and white Pye TV, a hand mower, a tent, a tartan quilt, a little basket containing three kittens, a tool kit, twelve volumes of an Encyclopaedia, a red scarf, a pair of Wellington boots, a bundle of old Women's Weekly magazines, two bedside lamps, the famous Rover 90, a purple pullover, a copy of a Margaret Fulton cook book, a fur coat, a Weber barbecue . . . .

When he saw the tears streaming down Lorna's face, Tom nodded briefly and the objects disappeared, the light faded and the music stopped.

"I recognised lots of those things," Bill murmured wistfully.

"I recognised all of them," Lorna said with determination. "They were all part of our life."

"It's a bit like that TV programme 'this is your life'", Bill added, thoughtfully.

Tim clapped happily. "Very good, very good. You see this cave represents your life, and the objects are things you have loved and discarded."

"We do create a lot of rubbish," Lorna concluded.

"And where do the tunnels go?" Bill asked, pointing to the openings he had just noticed.

"They take you to people you love," Tom explained. "The one on the far left goes to New Zealand . . ."

"Aunt Debby, we haven't seen her for a long time," Lorna said.

"The second one goes to Adelaide . . ."

"My brother Clive," Bill explained. "He's a bit of a pain in the butt, but he is my brother."

"And I bet the big one goes to the U.S.A.," Lorna concluded. "Our daughter, our grandchildren, we love them dearly."

"Don't neglect the tunnels of love," Tim recommended. "Travel them well and often."

"And keep away from doctors," Tom added. "Surgeries are dangerous places, full of sick people. You never know what you can catch when you go to the doctor."

Lorna laughed.

"Bill hates going to the doctor," she announced.

As there was nothing more to say, the two little men led them out of the cave and back towards their van. Bill turned round once, but the cave and the green light had disappeared.

Bill and Lorna hugged the two little men and watched them walk away across the field.

"I think I'll take a nap," Lorna said.

"Good idea," Tom replied. "I'll join you."

When they woke up, the sun was beginning to slide down towards the horizon.

"Better get on the way, "Tom suggested." I was hoping to stop in Strahan tonight."

"I had a funny dream," Lorna said. "It was about the family and leprechauns."

"Me too," Bill replied. "I'd like to invite my brother up for Easter. He must be feeling a little lonely since his wife died,"

"Good idea," Lorna approved.

"I thought we had broken down," she added, climbing into the front.

"Whatever gave you that idea?" Tom asked as he closed the door and fastened his seat belt.

"Must have been in my dream," Lorna murmured.

The engine started immediately Bill turned the key.

THE OLD LADY AND THE NEW WORLD

If a stressed and exhausted mother happened to sit in the doctor's waiting room with a bag containing throwaway plastic nappies, Alice would throw a fit. She believed firmly and loudly that the disposable nappy had destroyed the ozone layer and given birth to Bob Brown and the Green movement.

"In my time," she would say, "we made nappies out of towelling on a sewing machine. We washed them by hand with real soap and we put them out to dry on a clothes line. They dried thanks to what you idiots call solar and wind energy, and what we called nature."

The embarrassed mother would push her bag behind the chair, out of sight, and bury her face in Woman's Day. This would not discourage Alice. She hated those women who wandered around in Nike shoes, fluorescent tops and pants and who had a pony tail that danced as they walked.

"In my days we didn't have to go to a gym to work off fat," she would rumble. "We swept and polished, we washed and ironed, and we walked to the shops and back. Nowadays people run on a conveyor belt or ride a bike that goes nowhere. We were fit because we worked."

A red-faced pony tail would disappear behind Vogue magazine.

Alice hated the green shopping bags. She hated the disposable plastic bags too. If someone came into the waiting room with a green shopping bag, all hell would break loose.

"When I was young," Alice would announce loudly," we had shopping baskets. And if you had a lot of shopping to do, the shop would pack your purchases into large brown paper bags."

One day a lady tried to protest but was silenced.

"Those plastic bags go down our rivers into the sea where they choke the dolphins," Alice would explain. "That's why nowadays you see so many whales throw themselves on to the beaches. They've come to complain about the plastic bags."

Have you noticed the number of people who wander around with water in plastic bottles? Alice hated them!

"When I was a girl," she announced loudly, as a lady drank thirstily from her bottle," we drank from fountains and tap water from a glass. Nobody would have been stupid enough to pay a fortune for a plastic bottle full of tap water that's travelled halfway around the world."

The lady almost strangled herself in shame and left the waiting room coughing loudly.

"She'll probably throw the bottle in a gutter," Alice added spitefully as she left. "Then it will flow down our rivers to the sea . . . ."

"And choke the dolphins to death," a cantankerous old man added, hoping his interruption would make her shut up.

Alice glared.

"Look at the modern kitchens," Alice would complain to everybody in the room. "There are gadgets to slice, chop, peel, squeeze, crush, mix and spin. And the people who use them set up a demonstration to protest against the coal-fired power stations that make their little gadgets work."

Whoops! That one caused a few red faces.

"When my mother cooked dinner, she served us the vegetables of the season, she bought her meat from the butcher and her fish from the fishmonger," Alice explained one day. "Nowadays we have to eat frozen vegetables from China and Peru, asparagus from Bolivia, artichokes from Poland and God alone knows where the meat comes from."

Most people pretended not to listen, hoping that a lack of audience will discourage her. Not our Alice!

"And now we have these fast foods from America. People are too lazy to cook their own meals. Have you ever thought about the life of one of the Colonel's chickens? Nobody cares. We've all got cholesterol, high blood-pressure, diabetes and the parents need tanks weighing a couple of tons to get their fat kids to school. My neighbour's eight year old son looks like a Zeppelin, and I reckon his wife weighs as much as their Land Cruiser!"

It was spiteful and wicked, but there were a few unrestrained giggles. Giggling was the wrong thing to do, it only encouraged her.

"You idiots make me laugh when you talk about that new religion you've invented," Alice declared loudly one day to a packed waiting room. "'Recycling' you call it. We did that before you were born, but we didn't have to invent fancy words. The milkman brought us milk in glass bottles and we gave him back the empties to be washed and sterilised and re-used. We used to take the empty lemonade and ginger beer bottles back to the shop. I had a sister four years older than me and when she grew out of her clothes they were passed down to me. And when we had something fragile to send by parcel post we used to pack it in old newspapers."

She glared around the room, but nobody dared reply.

"Recycling!" she would snort. "It's your brains that need recycling!"

Nobody had seen Alice for quite a while, and when Ted went in for his monthly consultation with Kofi he asked if the doctor had seen her.

"She died three weeks ago," he told him, sadly.

"Was there a funeral?" he asked.

The doctor frowned. "Of course. Why do you ask?"

"I thought she might have been recycled," Ted explained.

Kofi laughed.

"Imagine a recycled Alice among us," he said with a grin.

"Totally organic," Ted assured him.